Harvey Angell

Beats Time

DIANA HENDRY BOOKS IN RED FOX

Harvey Angell
Harvey Angell and the Ghost Child
The Awesome Bird

Harvey Angell

BEATS TIME

DIANA HENDRY

RED FOX

for Hamish – with love

LINCOLNSHIRE
COUNTY COUNCIL

A Red Fox Book

Published by Random House Children's Books
20 Vauxhall Bridge Road, London SW1V 2SA

A division of The Random House Group Ltd
London Melbourne Sydney Auckland
Johannesburg and agencies throughout the world

3 5 7 9 10 8 6 4 2

First published in Great Britain by
Red Fox in 2000

The right of Diana Hendry to be identified as the
author of this work has been asserted by her in
accordance with the Copyright, Designs and Patents
Act, 1988.

The publishers gratefully acknowledge permission
to reprint 'The Blade' by Charles Tomlinson from
Annunciations published by Oxford University Press,
1989.

Printed and bound in Denmark by
Nørhaven

Papers used by Random House Group Ltd
are natural, recyclable products made from wood grown in
sustainable forests. The manufacturing processes conform to
the environmental regulations of the country of origin

The Random House Group Limited Reg. No. 954009

www.randomhouse.co.uk

ISBN 0 09 940447 8

Then
as I stood,
the shaft shifted,
fading across grass,
withdrew as visibly as the sand
down the throat of an hour-glass:
you could see time
trickle out, a grainy
lesion, and the green
filter back to fill
the crack in creation.

From 'The Blade'
by Charles Tomlinson

CHAPTER 1

It was two days after the Great Storm at the turn of the century that Henry found the bundle.

Ballantyre Road, where Henry lived, was still in a state of post-storm shock. Wheelie bins had skittered into the gutters. The sign board directing traffic to the city centre had folded itself up like a closed book. Ballantyre Road's two oaks and one sycamore looked as if they'd been knocked sideways in a boxing match with the wind.

Walking home from school, Henry had to step over tiles tossed off roofs, glass from shattered windows, several broken branches. One chimney pot rolled forlornly down the street. Another, like a king's lost crown, had come to rest by the postbox on the corner.

Henry was glad to get home. Apart from a blown down fence (wobbly even before the Great Storm), 131 Ballantyre Road had survived with its windows, roof and three chimney pots intact.

At first, closing the gate behind him, Henry

only saw that the hollyhocks which grew close to the front door had suddenly shot up. Surely yesterday they'd just been earth-hugging stumps waiting for summer? Now, as though January storms were what they thrived on, they were flowering.

Leafing and flowering as if they were trying to hide something. A cover-up operation was what Henry thought when he saw *what* they were hiding. A bundle. A bundle wrapped in a kind of white bubble wrap. A parcel dumped by the postman, was Henry's first guess. Rubbish blown there by the storm, his second.

But as he stared at it, a small pink shoot poked its way out of the bubble wrap and waved. Henry stood stock-still. He thought he might be seeing things. Perhaps a storm scattered the pictures in your mind, the way it scattered the leaves off trees. He closed his eyes, waited, opened them again. This time two pink plump shoots struggled out of the bubble wrap and at the end of each shoot were – yes, there definitely were – hands. Hands with tiny curled up fingers.

Henry knelt down by the hollyhocks. The bundle was quite firmly lodged within the thick hairy stems of the plants. Henry eased it out. The hollyhocks jiggled and joggled as if immensely pleased with themselves. As if, thought Henry, instead of growing another flower, they'd grown a baby.

CHAPTER 2

For that's what it was. Quite a small baby. A baby with bright blue eyes that gazed up trustingly into Henry's own brown ones.

In all his eleven years, Henry had never given more than a passing thought to babies. Of course he had friends at school with baby brothers or sisters. Henry's impression was that these lower beings were a considerable nuisance although, curiously, people loved them. He had vaguely noticed babies being pushed about in prams. They slept or they cried. Bald or bonneted, they all looked much of a muchness. If Henry had been asked to describe a baby he would have said it was a kind of blob waiting to take proper shape.

Very gingerly Henry lifted up this particular little blob. What he'd thought was bubble wrap, wasn't. It was some very soft, light material with tiny, insulating air pockets. Henry eased a little of the hood away from the blob's face as if to make absolutely sure it was a human child.

The baby had tiny frilled ears that reminded

him of buttercups. Did all babies have ears like this? Was this how ears began? Henry pulled up the hood again.

"Well, wherever did you come from?" Henry asked.

For answer the baby waved its arms at him. Automatically Henry put his finger into the baby's tiny hand and the baby gripped it fiercely. Henry grinned. Obviously this was an incredibly clever baby. It was unlike all others. (In this, at least, Henry was right.)

Henry stood on the path in the pale January sunshine that had followed the storm and wondered what to do next. The hollyhocks still jiggled and joggled. Celebrating. Henry's first instinct had been to rush into the house saying, 'Look what I've found!' but the thought of Aunt Agatha stopped him.

You could never guess what mood Aunt Agatha might be in. Henry thought Aunt Agatha herself probably couldn't guess it either. She just woke up one way or the other. Wintery or summery. Snappy or happy.

Long ago Aunt Agatha had had a baby of her own. Robin had died when he was only four and for many years grief had made Aunt Agatha mean and angry. In *that* mood Aunt Agatha could make leaves fall off trees and smiles fall off faces with one withering look. It was as if a permanent winter had set in her heart. It was like that in the house too. 131 Ballantyre Road, when Henry had first come to live there, was bleak and cold, a house haunted by sorrow.

The arrival of Harvey Angell had changed all that. And that was because Harvey Angell was a Homer. A Homer was a bit like an electrician but rather more like a magician and a Homer's job – Harvey Angell's job – was to turn unhappy houses into happy homes. When you learnt that this was done by *connecting the living and the dead* it all sounded very spooky indeed. But then you had to understand about the Circuit and the Energy Supply.

Everyone, Harvey Angell had told Henry, everyone from the long, long dead to the yet-to-be-born, was on the Circuit. And what kept everyone connected was the Energy – Energy that was a kind of love. Sorrow broke the Circuit and switched love off. A sorrow such as Aunt Agatha's. A sorrow that blocked the Energy, blocked out love. A sorrow that was catching, like the flu, and which had made everyone in 131 Ballantyre Road miserable.

That's how it had been until Harvey Angell arrived. He'd come with his silver flute, his Connecting Kit, his Energy Charger and his magical Centuries Clock to re-connect them to the Energy Supply. And that's what he'd done. He'd released the sorrow of the house. He'd sparked happiness into everyone – even Aunt Agatha.

But without Harvey Angell, without the sunshine of his 500 kilowatt smile, the music of his flute, the magic of his happy presence, Aunt

11

Agatha lapsed now and again. Lapsed into winter, as though winter was necessary to her. Henry knew that in a wintery mood, nobody, be it Queen, President or pop star, would be a welcome visitor to 131 Ballantyre Road. Least of all a baby.

Henry looked down at the bundle in his arms and wished Harvey Angell would appear. NOW. Sometimes he tried chanting Harvey Angell's rhyme in the hope that Harvey Angell would hear it and know that he was needed. He tried it now, very, very quietly:

"Watts and volts
Watts and volts
Better by far
Than thunderbolts."

Nothing happened. The bundle in his arms wriggled a little. It was a very warm bundle. Holding it was somehow comforting. "Don't worry about a thing," Henry told it, though he himself suddenly felt there was rather a lot to worry about.

Leaving his school bag on the front path, Henry tiptoed round to the back of the house. From across the road a window screeched open. Henry could feel the eyes of Mrs Sowerby watching him.

"She probably thinks I've stolen you," Henry told the bundle, for Mrs Sowerby seemed to watch, suspiciously, every coming and going at

131. "Mr Perkins," Henry whispered, close to the baby's buttercup ear. "That's who we need."

Mr Perkins was one of Aunt Agatha's three lodgers and, at this moment in time, the most useful one. The other two, Miss Muggins and Miss Skivvy, were mostly under Aunt Agatha's thumb. But Mr Perkins was in love with Aunt Agatha and had been known, on occasions, to charm her out of a winter mood and into mild spring. Mr Perkins was also a poet, though in Henry's opinion not a very good one. But somehow Henry hoped that being a poet-in-love might also mean that Mr Perkins had a soft spot for babies. Poets, love, babies, they seemed to go together nicely. At least in Henry's imagination.

Everything depended on Mr Perkins being up in his room working rather than lolling about the kitchen scoffing biscuits and complaining that the Muse had deserted him for the day.

As soon as he reached the back garden, Henry could see – with relief – that Mr Perkins *was* in his room. Not that he was working. The rather plump figure of Mr Perkins was framed in the window, juggling. When he saw Henry, Mr Perkins did one triumphant round of three balls, dropped them and shoved open the window.

"Henry!" he shouted. "What have you got there?"

"Ssssh!" hissed Henry. "You'll wake the baby!"

"Baby!" shouted Mr Perkins and then, seeing

the agonised look on Henry's face, hissed back, "Stay right there! I'm coming down!"

Keeping out of the way of the downstairs windows, Henry waited. He suddenly remembered that babies were meant to be rocked, so he did a little rocking. It was undoubtedly a very good baby he thought, because it didn't cry. Instead, standing in the silent garden, rocking and waiting for Mr Perkins, Henry distinctly heard a tiny "bleep . . . bleep . . . bleep!"

CHAPTER 3

"Babies don't bleep," whispered Mr Perkins.

"This one just did," Henry whispered back. The rocking had proved almost too successful. The baby had stopped bleeping and fallen asleep. "I found her under the hollyhocks," he added.

"Under the . . .? *Her*?" For once Mr Perkins was almost speechless.

"She looks like a she, don't you think?" said Henry. Mr Perkins peered into the baby's face. Henry thought he was never going to speak again. Eventually Mr Perkins hitched up his pyjama trousers (these being his special Poet-Pyjamas), cleared his throat and said, "What a darling!"

At that moment the back door flew open and Aunt Agatha appeared. "Perkins! Henry! What are you two doing out there?"

Henry and Mr Perkins exchanged desperate looks.

"The weather?" asked Henry, for this was

their way of exchanging vital information about Aunt Agatha's mood.

"Moderate to gale force winds," replied Mr Perkins. And then, to Aunt Agatha, "We've got something for you, dear!"

Henry trailed behind Mr Perkins. He found himself holding the bundle tightly as if to protect it from even moderate winds. "Don't bleep!" he whispered to the baby. "Just please don't bleep!"

Miss Muggins and Miss Skivvy were already in the kitchen when Mr Perkins, Henry-and-bundle appeared in the doorway. Miss Skivvy was peeling potatoes, Miss Muggins laying the table.

"Well?" snapped Aunt Agatha, "What is it?"

Mr Perkins stood aside so that she and Henry were face to face. Aunt Agatha's hair, usually swept up in swirls like an ice cream cornet, looked more like a badly made bird's nest. Bits of it stuck out, static with bad temper.

"I think . . ." began Henry nervously, "I think it's a baby!"

"You think it's a . . . What on earth d'you mean, child? Here! Let me look." Aunt Agatha peered inside the bundle as if afraid to touch the child inside it.

"Of course it's a baby," she said, so sharply that the baby at once opened its eyes. "Where did you get it, Henry? You must take it back straightaway!"

"I c-c-c-can't," stammered Henry. "You see, I found her . . ."

"We think she's been abandoned," put in Mr Perkins. He knew it wasn't the right moment (or mood) to mention the hollyhocks. Not yet, anyway.

"Here, give her to me," said Miss Muggins, taking the baby from Henry and seating herself in the old armchair Mr Perkins used when biscuit scoffing. Miss Muggins looked as instantly comfortable with the bundle as a violinist with his violin or a duck with a duckling. Everyone crowded round her as she undid the baby's airy white wrappings.

"Well!" cooed Miss Muggins, "isn't she a little dear?"

"A charmer," declared Miss Skivvy.

"She *is* rather nice," said Henry proudly.

"Smashing toes," said Mr Perkins tickling them.

"We must call the police," said Aunt Agatha.

Swiftly Miss Skivvy moved to put the kettle on. Mr Perkins eased Aunt Agatha into a chair and fetched a cardigan to put round her shoulders.

"Can't we keep her for just a little while?" asked Miss Muggins wistfully. "Just for a day or two?"

"Of course not!" snapped Aunt Agatha shrugging off the cardigan. "That baby belongs to someone. Besides, have you any idea what babies cost to keep, Muggins? Even for a day or two? There's nappies . . ."

"Nappies!" cooed Miss Muggins.

"Blankets, cots, prams," continued Aunt Agatha.

"Blankets, cots, prams," echoed Miss Skivvy practically and Miss Muggins longingly.

"Oh really!" cried Aunt Agatha. "You're both quite impossible. Perkins. Get on to the police."

"But what if no-one claims her?" asked Henry in a very small voice. The baby waved her arms at him as if she had already made her decision. She claimed Henry. Henry took her back from Miss Muggins. She nestled against his shoulder, snuggled into his neck.

There was a silence in the room as they all thought about children's homes, orphanages, unwanted babies. Henry remembered how he'd felt when his parents had been killed in the car accident and how, until Aunt Agatha appeared, he'd thought he'd be homeless.

Aunt Agatha looked down at the bundle in Henry's arms.

The baby attempted a smile. It was new and wobbly.

"Oh, the sweetheart!" they all (except Aunt Agatha) chorused.

"That's not our problem," said Aunt Agatha, turning away as if the smile hurt her. "Now, could one of you do something useful? We'll have to make some kind of crib for the child – until the police arrive that is. When I've had a good strong cup of tea, I'll call them myself."

Henry was left holding the baby while everyone else rushed around. Mr Perkins pulled

18

out a drawer from the bottom of the dresser. Miss Muggins produced blankets and an old, but delicate, shawl. Together they padded the drawer until it looked cosy as a bedroom slipper.

Before Aunt Agatha could take a first sip of her strong cup of tea, Miss Skivvy was down the road and back again with a basket full of nappies, talcum powder, bottles, teats, dried milk and a rattle.

(Mrs Sowerby, watching her come and go, was so agog she nearly fell out of her window.)

Mr Perkins set the crib-drawer across two chairs – "so she's not in a draught" – and Henry put the baby inside. Miss Muggins tucked the shawl round her.

"There you are, sweetheart," she said. "Snug as a bug in a rug."

"Sweetheart," said Henry. "Let's call her Sweetheart." And as if she agreed, the baby attempted a second wobbly smile.

Reluctantly Aunt Agatha came to look at Sweetheart in her crib. Ice, thought Henry. There's still some ice in Aunt Agatha and she's afraid of it cracking.

"Funny ears," said Aunt Agatha.

"Like buttercups," said Henry defensively.

"Odd she doesn't cry," said Aunt Agatha.

And at that moment two tiny antennae sprouted from Sweetheart's eyebrows – or where her eyebrows would be if she had any – and she began bleeping. The antennae were as tiny and delicate as those of a snail and they waved in the air as if Sweetheart was taking in the vibes of those about her, sensing their feelings.

"I'm definitely calling the police," said Aunt Agatha.

CHAPTER 4

"You can't," said Mr Perkins slamming his hand over the telephone just as Aunt Agatha reached it. "You really can't."

"That baby . . ." Aunt Agatha began, spluttering with temper, "that baby . . ."

"Sweetheart," corrected Mr Perkins.

"Is not a normal child," continued Aunt Agatha. "Do normal babies have buttercup ears? Do they bleep? Do they have antennae? No they do not." Aunt Agatha avoided looking at Sweetheart during this speech as if determined not to be won over by either smiles or bleeps. Indeed, Sweetheart's bleeps had reached a higher pitch and become as fast as an anxious alarm clock.

"All very good reasons why you can't phone the police," said Mr Perkins. "Sweetheart has been sent to us."

"Sent? Sent? Perkins, don't be so ridiculous," snapped Aunt Agatha. "By whom? And why?"

"That's what we've got to find out," said Mr Perkins adding an extra knot, like a final full stop, to the cord of his pyjamas.

It was then that Henry admitted it.

"I found her under the hollyhocks," he said.

There was a silence in the room. Over the years everyone who lived at 131 Ballantyre Road had become aware that there was something – if not exactly magical, then *knowing* – about the hollyhocks. When something was up, something about to happen, the hollyhocks became agitated, went into their jiggle-joggle mode. They had done so before the arrival of Harvey Angell. And while he stayed in the house, sleeping in the sloping-ceilinged attic that was now Henry's bedroom, they had grown new, white flowers – snowily white against the dark pink and purple of the existing blooms. When Harvey Angell went, the white hollyhocks went too as if, like him, they had just been visiting. Briefly. Magically.

"Under the hollyhocks," said Aunt Agatha, taking her hand off the telephone and sitting down again.

Miss Muggins had taken Sweetheart out of her crib and was rocking her again. The bleeps quietened to an occasional blip, much like a hiccup. Then Sweetheart found her thumb.

"Do you think," began Miss Muggins hesitantly, "that . . . that perhaps Harvey Angell sent her?"

"That's what we don't know," said Mr Perkins. "That's why we've got to look after her until we find out."

"Oh, all *right*!" said Aunt Agatha, as if it

wasn't all right at all, but all quite wrong. "But who's to look after her until we *do* find out?"

Four eager faces turned towards her. "I will," said Miss Muggins, Miss Skivvy, Mr Perkins and Henry all at once.

Aunt Agatha tugged at a few strands of her bird's nest hair and gave in. "Well, really," she said. "Two mothers, one father and a brother all in one go. Sweetheart's doing well."

"And what about you?" asked Mr Perkins. But Aunt Agatha only shivered a little and pulled on her cardigan.

* * *

But even though they had all – except Aunt Agatha – fallen in love with Sweetheart, she wasn't easy to look after. She did many of the things an ordinary baby does. She slept and woke. She weed and poohed. She waved her arms and curled her toes. She practised smiling. She gurgled but she didn't cry. They couldn't tell what she could hear through her buttercup ears and though they all felt her bleeps meant something, they didn't know exactly *what*. Her antennae (which, they had now decided, were very pretty), seemed to go in and out for no good reason at all. And worst of all was that they didn't know how to feed her.

Sweetheart would drink nothing but water. Lots of it. They tried cow's milk, goat's milk, soya milk and chocolate milk shake. They tried orange juice, rosehip and blackcurrant. Sweetheart wrinkled her nose and would have none of them.

They all worried about her obsessively. Mr Perkins devised a way of weighing her on the bathroom scales. First he weighed an old shopping basket that had lost its handle. Then he put Sweetheart in the basket and weighed both. Then he took away the weight of the shopping basket from the weight of Sweetheart + shopping basket and came up with 10lbs 2oz. And 10lbs 2oz was what Sweetheart was and what she stayed. She seemed perfectly content just on water.

They took it in turns – except you-know-who – to have Sweetheart in their rooms at night and though they all tried to be nice about it, there was considerable competition for Sweetheart's company.

There was something particularly nice about hearing Sweetheart sucking her thumb during the night, hearing her tiny bleeps and gurgles. And something even nicer about waking up in the morning to find Sweetheart in her crib, blankets kicked away, pedalling the air with her chubby legs while showing off a most kissable tum.

Henry was allowed to have Sweetheart in his room more than the others because, as he reminded everyone, "I found her", and because, Aunt Agatha said, having Sweetheart in his room woke him nice and early for school. And lastly because Mr Perkins' habit of pacing the floor and reciting poems during the night was not, according to Aunt Agatha, healthy. Mr Perkins disagreed and said that an early knowledge of English literature was very good for babies and they should have poems mixed in with their cereals. But Aunt Agatha only said, "Piffle!"

Apart from how to feed Sweetheart, there were other problems. They bathed her in the kitchen sink and Miss Skivvy bought a second-hand pram from an advert in the local paper. This meant that Sweetheart could be put out in the garden and get a dose of fresh air. But they worried about other people seeing her. Seeing her buttercup ears and the antennae they had now grown so used to that some days Miss Muggins would stroke them with her little finger.

The problem of Sweetheart's ears was easily resolved. Aunt Agatha, while saying firmly that she was not going to become 'Mumsy and besotted' like others in the house, nevertheless went out and bought three bonnets. They were such plain bonnets that Mr Perkins immediately went to the best baby shop in town and bought the prettiest bonnet he could find, complete with pink silk ribbons and embroidered with rosebuds.

"That," said Aunt Agatha, "is the most sentimentally soppy bonnet I have ever seen." But she kissed Mr Perkins on the top of his head which was something she had never, ever been known to do before.

Sweetheart had that kind of effect on people. They all became a little kinder to each other and the world in general. Henry found himself helping worms across the wide stoney paths of the park. Miss Skivvy took to bringing everyone a morning cup of tea. She did it briskly and loudly and the tea was very strong but no-one complained. Aunt Agatha, for whom meanness had become as much a part of her character as the worry lines on her forehead, cooked extra potatoes at supper time and, on an exceptionally chilly night, actually turned up the heating, saying, "Just for Sweetheart, of course. We can't have her catching a cold."

Once Henry caught Aunt Agatha leaning over Sweetheart's crib and stroking her cheek. Kissing and cuddling seemed too difficult for Aunt Agatha but, as Mr Perkins whispered to Henry, her mood-weather was "mild, getting warmer."

Miss Muggins knitted and knitted and knitted. Vests. Cardigans. Shawls. Bootees. They fell off her needles faster than rain down a train window. Mr Perkins' baby poems were stuck all over the bathroom wall. They were even more sentimentally soppy than the rosebud bonnet. One of them read:

> She's my Sweetheart,
> She's my girl,

26

She's my honey-bun,
She's my pearl.
She's my geranium,
She's my jewel,
She's my princess,
I'm her fool.

"Why 'geranium'?" asked Henry.

"Because I am very fond of them," said Mr
Perkins defensively. "They brighten my life, like
Sweetheart does. Anyway, I needed it for the
rhythm."

"The last line is certainly true," said Aunt
Agatha.

"A fool, in Shakesperian terms, is a very wise
man," said Mr Perkins loftily.

"Obviously there are exceptions," said Aunt
Agatha. "And what's with this 'my'? I hope you
haven't forgotten that we are waiting for
Whoever-it-is who sent Sweetheart to come and
collect her?"

Although none of them said so, they had all
come to believe that Sweetheart had been sent
by Harvey Angell. Harvey Angell had freed Ballantyre Road of sorrow. On holiday in Scotland
they had called on him to resolve the mystery of
the ghost child haunting the house they'd rented.
They thought of him as almost one of the family,
or at least a distant and very special relative.
"Our Mr Angell" was how Miss Muggins and
Miss Skivvy spoke of him, much as Mr Perkins
now spoke of "my" Sweetheart. That Harvey

Angell had sent Sweetheart to them to look after seemed to them the only explanation for her arrival.

So they waited and watched the hollyhocks for clues. But one week went by, then two and there was no sign of Harvey Angell.

"Held up somewhere," Mr Perkins said to Henry. "On one of his Homing Missions. Harvey Angell's idea of time isn't the same as ours, you know."

"Of course I know," said Henry. (He was remembering Harvey Angell's clock that told the time not in hours and minutes, but in years and centuries.) "Past, present and future are all one to Mr Angell."

"Umm," agreed Mr Perkins. They were sitting in the kitchen with Sweetheart between them watching a mobile of cardboard fishes Henry had made and hung from the ceiling.

"I expect he'll come when he can," said Mr Perkins, "our Mr Angell. He'll come or he'll send word."

But the days went by and there was still no Harvey Angell. Instead Ballantyre Road suddenly acquired a great many other visitors. Not all of them nice ones. The hollyhocks grew strange green flowers with coal-black middles and they didn't so much jiggle and joggle as shiver.

CHAPTER 5

Rosie Brock was the first visitor and Rosie was OK. Rosie was a baby addict. She lived in the street at the back of Ballantyre Road and had spotted the pram in the garden.

"Rosie would spot a pram a million miles away," said Aunt Agatha.

Rosie was ten and no-one knew why she was so keen on babies. Perhaps because she had no brothers or sisters, or perhaps because she was in training for a career as a baby-sitter, or perhaps because, as Mr Perkins said, "she collects baby smiles like other people collect stamps".

Whatever the reason, Rosie had a way of making even the most gloomy baby smile. It could have been the way her ginger plaits, tied with red and green bobbles, dangled temptingly over a pram. Or it could have been her own smile which was big and wide and topped with sparky brown eyes. Babies smiled at Rosie like they smiled at no-one else, and Rosie smiled at them.

Rosie didn't knock at the door of 131 or wait for an invitation. (She would have had a long wait.) Rosie simply climbed over the wall one Saturday morning and Henry found her there leaning over Sweetheart's pram and with Sweetheart clutching one of Rosie's ginger plaits while Rosie did 'this little piggy' with Sweetheart's toes.

"And this little piggy went wee wee wee, all the way home," Rosie finished as Henry appeared.

Sweetheart was wearing one of the plain Aunt Agatha bonnets so her ears were hidden. She was too busy playing with Rosie's plait to bleep, and for the time being her antennae had retracted so that all you could see were two tiny little red pin heads just above her eyes. Even so, Henry was worried.

"Hello," said Rosie. "Is she your sister?"

Henry was stuck. He didn't want to lie and he couldn't tell the truth. By now Sweetheart *felt* like his sister, indeed he thought of her as Little Sis. So now he said, "Well, sort of."

Rosie Brock laughed. "Hello, sort-of-sister," she said.

"Her name's Sweetheart," said Henry putting a proprietary hand on the pram's handle.

"You're very lucky," sighed Rosie. "I'd love a little sister or brother but my mum can't have any more, so there's just me."

Out of sympathy for this state of affairs, Henry felt obliged to tell Rosie just a little of the truth.

"Well, she's not really ours," he said. "We've just got her on – on loan."

"Like a library book," said Rosie, laughing again. "And if you keep her too long you get a fine."

Henry laughed too. Perhaps it was the laughter that did it. Sweetheart let go of Rosie's plait and out came her antennae.

"Oh look!" said Rosie. "What dear little feelers. Do you think it makes her telepathic?"

"Telly-what?" asked Henry.

"Telepathic," repeated Rosie. "It means being able to read other people's thoughts. Probably she can sense things with them that we can't. I think that's awfully clever."

Rosie spoke as if Sweetheart was somehow an improved version of ordinary babies.

Henry, who until now had not thought much of Rosie Brock, now decided she was very OK. Possibly brilliant. She hadn't been shocked by Sweetheart's antennae. She approved of them. Henry thought he might offer Rosie his new, luminous yo-yo. He realised too that they'd all felt so embarrassed by Sweetheart's antennae that none of them had questioned what they might be for. Sweetheart's 'feelers', Henry decided, standing there in the rather neglected back garden, were something they should all be proud of.

"I'd better go," said Rosie. "But can I come and visit? I'm quite good at looking-after. Mum says I've a talent for it."

"Yes," said Henry, feeling grandly generous, "come any time."

"Perhaps if you're a sort-of-brother, I could be a sort-of-sister," suggested Rosie.

This was pushing it. "Maybe," said Henry. "But you see Sweetheart's already got two mothers and . . ."

But Rosie was already off, over the wall. He heard a thump as she landed, an "Ooops!" and a fading "byyyyeee!"

* * *

So Rosie was all right, but the women who began knocking at the door of 131 Ballantyre Road and asking to see Sweetheart were much more worrying.

Two came on Monday. Three on Wednesday and Thursday. None on Friday.

"They've given up," said Aunt Agatha with relief. But they hadn't. There were two more on Saturday.

"They give me the creeps," said Mr Perkins. "They're so skinny a puff of wind could blow them over. And they look so mournful."

"All dressed in black," said Aunt Agatha, "it's most disturbing."

"I feel sorry for them," said Miss Skivvy. "They look so sad. But you must admit they're very polite."

This was true. Some of the women were young, some old. One or two wore veils over

32

their faces. Their voices were strangely echoey, but they all asked the same question – "May I see the child please?"

And somehow it was impossible to refuse.

"After all," said Aunt Agatha, "one of them might be Sweetheart's mother. How are we to know?"

"And how do *they* know she's here?" asked Mr Perkins. None of them could answer that and all of them hoped that Sweetheart's mother (if she had one) *wasn't* one of the strange black-clad ladies.

Mr Perkins tried asking one or two of them if, perhaps, they knew of a certain Mr Angell. But they looked at him blankly. Besides, they had eyes – rather hungry eyes, Henry thought nervously – for no-one but Sweetheart. They came into the kitchen. They gazed at Sweetheart as if she was the loveliest creature they had ever seen. If Sweetheart was in her crib they knelt down beside it. Each one of them wept a little, shook her head and went away.

"Without so much as a thank-you," said Aunt Agatha crossly.

But Miss Muggins took to buying boxes of paper tissues to hand out at the front door.

"Witchy," said Mr Perkins come Sunday, when ten of the dark women had called, looked hungrily at Sweetheart, wept and gone.

"Don't be silly, Perkins," said Aunt Agatha, "there are no such things as witches any more."

"Anyway," said Miss Skivvy, "if they were witches they'd have cats and broomsticks."

"And spells," said Miss Muggins. "You don't hear any of them muttering a spell, do you?"

And they had to agree they didn't. But although none of the women cast an actual spell on Sweetheart, they did cast a silent kind of spell over everyone in 131.

"It's like having a kind of funeral procession going through the house," grumbled Mr Perkins. "Have you noticed how you can't hear their footsteps?"

"They don't so much walk as – as float," said Miss Muggins with a shiver.

"It can't be good for Sweetheart," said Mr Perkins.

"She doesn't seem to mind," said Henry. "In fact mostly she just smiles at them."

"Well, they make *me* feel like crying," said Mr Perkins.

It was Rosie Brock who sorted things out, though that wasn't until there was almost a queue of dark women waiting at the door every morning as soon as it was light.

CHAPTER 6

Henry had not anticipated that telling Rosie she could come "any time" meant that she would come, if not quite *all* the time, then certainly every day.

Rosie came before school and after school and most of Saturday and Sunday. It was Rosie who discovered that Sweetheart would drink the water in which vegetables had been boiled. Carrot water, cabbage water, leek water even potato water. The discovery delighted Aunt Agatha who suggested that they should all try this instead of tea and coffee and that it would be very good for them. ("Not to mention very cheap," muttered Mr Perkins.) Sweetheart would also take – from the tip of Rosie's little finger – a tiny lick of honey.

They were jubilant. Sweetheart's weight went up two ounces in just one week and any doubts they had about having Rosie around were quickly quashed.

At first they'd all been rather cross with Henry for inviting Rosie in.

"Well, she sort of invited herself," protested Henry. (Lots of things in life were "sort-of" to Henry.)

"She'll ask questions," said Mr Perkins.

"She'll hear the bleeps," said Miss Muggins, "and see Sweetheart's antennae."

"She's already seen them," said Henry. "She calls them 'feelers'. She thinks Sweetheart might be telly-bottic."

"You mean telepathic," said Mr Perkins. "Um, an interesting thought."

"Obviously an intelligent girl," said Aunt Agatha, "so we must be sure we all tell her the same story."

"What is it?" they all asked together.

"That we are looking after Sweetheart for Mr Angell and that she is here on – on holiday. But that we are under instructions not to tell anyone about her."

So that's what Rosie was told.

"But who *is* Mr Angell?" Rosie asked Henry.

"He's an old friend," Henry said, "a very special old friend." (A magical friend, he was thinking.)

"And what about *Mrs* Angell?" asked Rosie. "Is she an old friend too?"

"I don't think there *is* a Mrs Angell," said Henry, to which Rosie replied, "Don't be silly, Henry. Even if there isn't a Mrs Angell, Sweetheart must have a mother. Everyone has one."

It was a Saturday morning and they were taking Sweetheart to the park in her pram.

These days they felt Sweetheart was safer outside, away from the dark women, than she was at home. The pram was large and old. It had a big grey hood which successfully muffled Sweetheart's bleeps should she be in bleeping mode. The rosebud bonnet hid her ears. That left only her feelers to worry about and Henry and Rosie had developed the knack of hurrying past anyone who looked as if they wanted to stop and admire Sweetheart.

Mr Perkins was in the park already, standing on a soap box and giving a recital of his Aunt Agatha love poems to an audience of three. Beside him was a signboard that read 'PETER PERKINS. PERFORMANCE POET.'

"What an embarrassment," said Henry. "Let's take the other path."

"I suppose we can't tell anyone about Sweetheart because she's so special," said Rosie as they took it in turns to push the pram.

"We've had instructions," said Henry, "not to tell anyone."

"Whose instructions?" asked Rosie.

Henry nearly said, 'Aunt Agatha's' but stopped himself in time. "That's a secret too," he said.

"Well, it's not much of one," said Rosie. "What about those women who come asking to see Sweetheart? How do they know about her?"

They had reached the swings and slides. "You can go first," said Henry, "while I look after Sweetheart." (That was the arrangement. One swung or slid, the other watched over Sweetheart.)

"Well how?" persisted Rosie. "How do those women know?"

"Maybe they're friends of Mr Angell," said Henry, although he didn't for one minute believe this.

"Ha!" said Rosie, running for the swings, "Very funny friends!"

★ ★ ★

And indeed they were. They had all come to dread the knock on the door and the sight, on the doorstep, of what Mr Perkins called 'another witchy one'. As the numbers grew, Henry would wake up in the morning, look through his attic window and see a queue of them forming down the path and along Ballantyre Road. He noticed too that when the women appeared, the weird black and green hollyhocks closed up, held themselves very still and looked as if they were trying to shrink.

When the women came into the house it was as if they made the warmest room chilly, the brightest day dark. The gloom they left behind them was like a fall of soot. One or two of the women were so thin Henry thought he could almost see through them. Several were toothless. Henry noticed that seen outside, in the sunlight, none of them had shadows. Worst of all was the fact that the women themselves appeared to see no-one but Sweetheart.

"It's as if we don't exist," said Mr Perkins, and when he said this Henry had to go and look at himself in the mirror just to make sure he did.

"Why don't we just say, 'not today, thank you' and close the door on them?" asked Mr Perkins.

"Because," said Aunt Agatha, "firstly, we can't be sure Sweetheart doesn't belong to one of them . . ."

"She can't! She just can't!" cried Henry, for he couldn't bear the thought of one of the witchy ones taking Sweetheart away.

Aunt Agatha held up her hand. "And secondly," she continued, "because we don't know what they'd do if we shut them out."

(Since the coming of the dark women, Aunt Agatha had become fiercely protective of Sweetheart. She had taken to checking up on her in the middle of the night, sometimes singing a lullaby as if a song would keep Sweetheart safe.)

"So you *do* think they're witches," said Mr Perkins.

"Perkins, I don't know *who* they are," said Aunt Agatha. "All I'm saying is that where Sweetheart is concerned we can't afford to take any risks. But I wish they'd all go away and never come back."

Henry wished it too. Only Miss Muggins and Rosie took a different view. Miss Muggins and Rosie had begun calling the women "the Poor

Witchy Dears". Miss Muggins couldn't resist anyone who cried and the Poor Witchy Dears did a lot of that. As for Rosie, she saw the women as baby-addicts-without-babies. Nevertheless it was Rosie who put things on a practical footing – or, as Mr Perkins said, "arranged a Witch Watch".

"We can't have them turning up at all hours of the day and night," said Rosie.

"But what can we do about it?" asked Miss Muggins.

"We put a notice on the door saying, 'Viewing: by appointment only. Between the hours of four and six p.m.'" said Rosie.

"What if everyone's out?" asked Aunt Agatha.

"We have a rota," said Rosie. "One of us is always on duty so we can keep an eye on the Poor Witchy Dears.

"And on Sweetheart," added Miss Muggins.

Henry noticed how Rosie had taken to speaking of "we" and "us" as if she was one of the family. But he didn't mind. Henry had changed his own mind. Not only about babies but about girls too. Particularly Rosie.

They wrote the notice together, chosing pink ink because Rosie said they needed a cheerful colour. Rosie did the writing and Henry added a decorative border of flowers – they looked vaguely like hollyhocks – and baby bonnets. Mr Perkins nailed it to the front door.

Suddenly the house became peaceful again. Instead of the constant knocking on the door, there was just the sound of calling cards plopping through the letter box.

'Wilhemina will call Wednesday, 4 p.m.' said one. 'Expect Mabel on Friday, 5.15 p.m.' said another. 'Ephemia will call on Thursday at 4.30 sharp,' said a third.

"At least they've now got names," said Mr Perkins, even if they haven't got shadows."

Rosie pinned up a rota in the kitchen. It looked like this:

Monday	Aunt Agatha
Tuesday	Mr Perkins
Wednesday	Half day closing
Thursday	Henry
Friday	Miss Skivvy
Saturday	Miss Muggins & Rosie
Sunday	Henry and Mr Perkins.

The combination of limited visiting hours and Rosie's rota made them all feel a bit easier – more as if they were in control and not 'taken over by dark forces' as Mr Perkins put it.

But hardly had they relaxed a little when another visitor arrived. This one was very brightly coloured and paid no attention to the notice on the door.

CHAPTER 7

It was Mrs Sowerby. Mrs Sowerby dressed for battle. Her coat, like a soldier's, had brass buttons all down the front. Her bright red hat was held on by a hatpin fierce as a miniature sword. Beneath the hat, Mrs Sowerby's eyes were equally fierce and stabbing.

It was a Sunday morning. Miss Muggins opened the door and Mrs Sowerby swept past her like a bomber jet certain of its destination – which was the kitchen. Miss Muggins was left standing at the door with her mouth opening and closing on a 'hello'.

Mrs Sowerby's eyes mine-swept the room. She saw Mr Perkins biscuiting in his pyjamas; Aunt Agatha at the table with her big black accounts book in front of her; Miss Skivvy strangely sieving potato water into bottles, and Henry and Rosie sitting on the floor, apparently besotted by the contents of a large old drawer.

"Mrs Sowerby!" said Aunt Agatha, attempting her sweetest tone (never easy and less so when in mid-sum), "How nice of you to call!"

"Spells, I suppose!" exploded Mrs Sowerby, gesturing at the big black accounts book. "And potions!" she added, pointing an accusing finger at Miss Skivvy. Aunt Agatha closed her accounts book. Miss Skivvy spilt the potato water.

"Do sit down, Mrs Sowerby," said Aunt Agatha. "You're obviously very upset."

"I'll not sit down in this house," said Mrs Sowerby, holding herself very erect so that the brass buttons seemed to blaze at them and the hatpin quivered with the hope of action. Two blotches, red as her hat, appeared on Mrs Sowerby's cheeks.

"This is a house of black magic," she pronounced. "You should all be thrown out of the neighbourhood. Thrown out!" she repeated.

Mr Perkins, scattering biscuits crumbs (some down his pyjama trousers), stood up.

"My dear lady," he began.

"Don't you 'dear lady' me", said Mrs Sowerby backing away. "I've seen you in the park chanting spells, inciting people to passion . . ."

"Did you think so?" said Mr Perkins, rather flattered. "Of course I know some of my poems are considered quite strong but . . ."

"Perkins! Be quiet!" instructed Aunt Agatha. Mr Perkins subsided. Henry and Rosie choked on their giggles. In her drawer at the back of the kitchen, Sweetheart slept peacefully.

43

"Now, Mrs Sowerby," continued Aunt Agatha, "please try and tell me what has upset you so much?"

"Those women," said Mrs Sowerby. "A queue of them last week. All in black. All down the road. That's what's upset me."

"Oh, you mean the Poor Witchy Dears," said Miss Skivvy before she could stop herself.

Aunt Agatha waved Miss Skivvy silent.

"See!" cried Mrs. Sowerby, "That's a confession if ever I heard one. Witches. Not just witches. Witchy *dears*! I knew it. I knew it in my bones and quite obviously you're all in league with them."

"It's not what it seems!" cried Henry and then wished he hadn't, for Mrs Sowerby marched across the kitchen and stood looking down – with alarm and astonishment – at Sweetheart in her crib-drawer.

Maybe it was the brightness of Mrs Sowerby's hat or maybe – as Rosie claimed later – it was Sweetheart's telepathic powers beginning to work, but Sweetheart woke at once. Out came her feelers. The bleeping was louder than they'd ever heard before.

Mrs Sowerby screamed. Words clearly failed her. Wild-eyed she rushed from the kitchen and it wasn't until she reached the front door that she recovered her voice enough to shout, "I'm calling the police! Now!" Then the door banged behind her.

Rosie picked Sweetheart up and rocked her calm again.

"Now what?" asked Aunt Agatha.

"We hide her," said Miss Skivvy. "Or no, we *all* go into hiding." (Miss Skivvy felt quite excited by the idea. She had an adventurous spirit, but lacked opportunity.)

"Not very practical," said Aunt Agatha. "And have you somewhere in mind?"

"Scotland. We could go back to Scotland," said Miss Skivvy eagerly.

"To Sibbald House," said Henry, remembering their holiday in the ramshackle old house by the sea.

Aunt Agatha sighed. "Running away would just arouse even greater suspicions," she said. "Anyway, I doubt we have time."

"Well, what *are* we going to do?" asked Miss Muggins. It was more of a bleat than a question.

"No-one's going to take Sweetheart away," said Henry fiercely. Mr Perkins put an arm round Henry's shoulders. Rosie gave his hand a squeeze.

"We don't know anything about the Poor Witchy Dears, do we?" said Aunt Agatha slowly. "I mean we don't know who they are or why they want to see Sweetheart."

This was agreed. "In fact," said Aunt Agatha, "we'd be quite grateful if the police stopped them coming, wouldn't we?" This too was agreed. "So that's what we tell the police," said Aunt Agatha.

"Only we're very careful not to call them witchy," said Mr Perkins.

"Agreed," they chorused.

"But what about Sweetheart?" asked Rosie. "What if her feelers pop out? What if she bleeps at the police like she did at Mrs Sowerby?"

"My inclination," said Aunt Agatha, "is to trust Sweetheart to know what's best."

"Wow!" said Rosie, "So *you* think she's telepathic too?"

"I'm not saying that I do or don't," said Aunt Agatha carefully, "but . . ."

But whatever Aunt Agatha was about to say next was interrupted by the sight of a panda car drawing up outside 131 and two policemen stepping out of it.

"Thank goodness it's not the afternoon for Wilhemina, Mabel or Euphemia," said Mr Perkins. "Or any of the others."

"Perkins, I wish you weren't in pyjamas," said Aunt Agatha. "And is Sweetheart wearing her bonnet?"

"She is now," said Rosie.

* * *

There was one old policeman, PC 45 and one young, well-scrubbed one, PC 16. They removed their hats as they came in. PC 45 asked the questions. PC 16 wrote down the answers in his notebook.

"We've had reports," said the older

46

policeman, rocking on his heels a little, "of incidents calculated to disturb the peace." He gave an embarrassed cough, "Er, something to do with witches and an alien baby. I'm sure we can clear this up without any fuss. It all sounds most unlikely. I think you might have a very imaginative neighbour."

(Little did either policeman know about the over-active imaginations of the occupants of 131 Ballantyre Road, nor that ever since she'd been caught, as a girl, stealing apples from an orchard, Miss Muggins was terrified of policemen.)

"These so-called witches," began PC 45, "have you observed them about your property?"

"Observed them?" squeaked Miss Muggins, "We're haunted by them night and day."

('Haunted night and day,' wrote PC 16.)

"There's Wilhemina, Mabel, Euphemia and – and, well there's hundreds of them. Maybe thousands," jittered Miss Muggins. "Thousands," she repeated, "all in black. Day and night."

(In fairness to Miss Muggins it has to be said that when she pictured the PWDs, the queue of them grew in her mind. Stretched down the road and round the corner, on and on and on.)

PC 16 was struggling to spell Wilhemina and Euphemia.

"Oh, so you know some of them by name, do you?" said PC 45. He was looking less affable. Aunt Agatha groaned. "We don't know where

47

they come from and we rather hope you might put a stop to – to their activities," said Aunt Agatha as firmly as she could.

"Yes," broke in Miss Muggins, "because I hate being on the rota you know. I hate it. I hate it." Miss Skivvy trod very firmly on Miss Muggins' toes, but Miss Muggins didn't even notice.

"The rota?" queried PC 45.

"For when they visit?" burbled Miss Muggins, now as out of control as a burst pipe from which water gushes and gushes unstoppably.

('Rota for visiting witches,' wrote PC 16 and then crossed out 'witches' and wrote 'ladies'.)

"And we're very frightened they want to take our baby," finished Miss Muggins in a final gush.

Aunt Agatha gave up. She sat down at the kitchen table with her head in her hands.

"Ah yes, now, the baby," said PC 45. "We have a description of her here." He turned to the young policeman who flicked back several pages in his notebook, cleared his throat and began reading.

"Very strange, ugly child . . ." he read.

"She is *not*!" cried Henry. "She's beautiful!"

"Cosmic," murmured Rosie.

PC 45 held up his hand. PC 16 continued. "With snail-like feelers. Has internal bleeper and horrible eyes."

"They're lovely eyes!" said Henry. He could feel his own burning with tears.

"Don't get all worked up, lad," said PC 45 "Perhaps we can have a look at this baby."

"She's asleep," said Henry.

"Asleep or awake we can still look."

"Let them look, Henry," said Aunt Agatha wearily.

"She's here, Sweetheart's here," said Henry pointing to the drawer.

"Got her in a box then, have you?" said PC 45.

"It's a drawer," said Mr Perkins, "and a very comfy drawer."

Both policeman bent down to look. Sweetheart slept on. She didn't bleep. She didn't pop a feeler. They all agreed later that she had never looked so angelic.

"Umm," said PC 45, "she looks like any other baby to me."

"I can see why you call her Sweetheart," said PC 16 and blushed.

"Yes, Sweetheart," repeated PC 45. "Is that her proper name would you say, or just a nickname?"

"It's her *only* name," said Henry.

Another gush of words was welling up in Miss Muggins. "You see when she came we didn't know what else to call her and so . . ." Aunt Agatha managed to quell her with a look.

('Proper name: Sweetheart,' recorded P.C. 16.)

"When she came . . .?" prompted PC 45. Henry couldn't help noticing that the constable's voice was growing heavier and heavier as if weighed down by suspicion. "So she isn't your child, this Sweetheart?" continued PC 45. He looked sternly at Miss Muggins. "And you were about to tell me where she came from, weren't you?"

Miss Muggins panicked. Blinked. Swallowed. Burst. "She didn't come from anywhere, I mean of course she came from *somewhere* but we didn't steal her, if that's what you mean. It wasn't like the apples in the orchard. No, not at all. We'd never do anything like that. Ever. No, she was just there, under the hollyhocks and . . ."

('Found under the hollyhocks,' wrote PC 16.)

Aunt Agatha put a hand on Miss Muggins' shoulder. "That will do, Muggins," she said gently, and to PC 45, "Please excuse her, officer. It's her nerves, you know. She really doesn't know what she's saying."

"That's true," agreed Miss Muggins hastily. "I never know what I'm saying. Never. Particularly not now. Things just pop out."

"Like babies from under hollyhocks or babies delivered by stork," said PC 45.

"Yes, just like that," said Miss Muggins relieved that at last she was understood.

"So would *you* care to enlighten us?" said PC 45 turning to Aunt Agatha.

"Sweetheart belongs to an old friend of ours," said Aunt Agatha, "and we are looking after her for him." They had all thought this for so many weeks that Aunt Agatha now firmly believed it.

"And his name, ma'am?" PC 16 held his pencil poised.

"Mr Angell. Mr Harvey Angell," said Aunt Agatha.

('Sweetheart's father an angel,' wrote PC 16.)

"And an address, please?"

"Ah, that's more difficult," said Aunt Agatha. "I think at this moment in time, Mr Angell has no fixed abode. That's it. No fixed abode."

"Might it be heaven?" suggested PC 45.

('Heaven,' wrote PC 16 then crossed it out.)

It was Aunt Agatha's turn to blush. "No, of course not, officer. It's just that at the moment we don't know Mr Angell's whereabouts."

"Even though you're looking after his daughter?" said PC 45.

"I didn't say it was his daughter," hedged Aunt Agatha.

"His niece maybe? Or his fifth cousin three times removed," suggested PC 45.

"I admit we don't know exactly," Aunt Agatha floundered, "but she's certainly a close – a close relative."

"Seems to me there's rather a lot you don't know *exactly*," said PC 45. "We may have to investigate further. May have to send in Social Services. Put this – this Sweetheart into care until this angel of yours turns up."

PC 16 closed his notebook, chucked

Sweetheart under the chin while PC 45 wasn't looking, and then both policemen left.

In the kitchen there was an awful silence broken only when Miss Muggins started crying. "I'm sorry, I'm sorry, I'm sorry," sobbed Miss Muggins. "I just couldn't stop myself."

"So we noticed," said Aunt Agatha grimly

"There, there, dear," said Miss Skivvy feeling guilty about stamping on Miss Muggins' toes.

Henry had picked Sweetheart up, even though she was asleep, and was holding her tight as if expecting her to be taken from him at any moment. "Little Sis," he murmured into Sweetheart's bonneted, buttercup ear, "dear Little Sis."

"Henry," said Mr Perkins, with sudden authority accompanied by a pulling tight of his pyjama cord, "Henry, you know what we have to do, don't you?"

Henry looked across the kitchen at Mr Perkins. A Mr Perkins who had lost his dreamy-poet look. A plumply positive Mr Perkins. A Mr Perkins In Charge. And looking at him Henry suddenly caught, by telepathy, the thought that Mr Perkins sent winging across the kitchen.

Henry stopped looking miserable and grinned.

"Yes!" he said. "Yes, I DO know!"

CHAPTER 8

"We've to find Harvey Angell," said Henry.

"Spot on," said Mr Perkins.

They were out in the back garden, Mr Perkins insisting that they needed peace and quiet for a Summit Meeting.

"It's a meeting for people with summat important to discuss," said Mr Perkins loftily. "Which is what Henry and I are now going to do."

"Don't be silly," said Rosie. " 'Summit' means 'the top'. Mountains have summits and top people like prime ministers and presidents have Summit Meetings."

"Same difference," said Mr Perkins who at the moment was feeling fairly prime ministerial himself.

So now Henry and Mr Perkins sat on a big log at the end of the garden and Rosie hovered at the back door.

"I've got summat to say too!" shouted Rosie. "You shouldn't leave your friends out of things.

Particularly when they could be useful. That's U-S-E-F-U-L."

"I know how to spell 'useful'," shouted Mr Perkins.

"Perhaps we could let her join in," said Henry.

"Can we trust her?" asked Mr Perkins. "We'd have to explain about Harvey Angell."

"I'd trust her with Sweetheart's life," said Henry.

"Enough said," said Mr Perkins and he waved Rosie over.

She squatted in front of them, her ginger plaits bobbing with every nod of her head.

"But *how* do we find him?" asked Henry. "And *where*?"

"I suppose you're talking about this Mr Angell of yours," said Rosie.

"I'd have you know, young Rosie, that Mr Angell is a very special kind of person." Mr Perkins paused, trying to think how to explain the magical, the inspiring nature of Harvey Angell. "He's what you might call a Bright Spark in everyone's life," he continued. "So I'd ask you to speak his name with the deepest respect. The deepest."

Rosie raised her eyebrows and said nothing, though privately she was thinking 'phooey!'

"When we were in Scotland, we wrote to him," said Henry, "and he came."

"In a helicopter like a jewelled silver dragonfly," Mr Perkins recalled dreamily.

"Are you sure he didn't jump out of a bottle like a genie?" asked Rosie.

It was Henry's turn to feel cross. "I don't understand you," he said. "It's not as if you're against magic. It's you who thinks Sweetheart's telly-whatsit. You don't mind her having fantastical ears and fantastical antennae, but you won't believe what we tell you about Harvey Angell."

Rosie turned red and sulky, dug the heel of her trainers in the soil and began to defend herself. "I believe in evolution, not magic," she said. "Sweetheart's – well, she's kind of cosmic. A cosmic baby, that's what. I think she's the child of the future. So there! That's what I think and you can like it or lump it."

"Well," said Mr Perkins, trying to patch things up, "maybe evolution's magic and magic's evolutionary."

"We've no time for all this," said Henry impatiently. "They could come and take Sweetheart away unless we do something. We *need* Harvey Angell and we need him fast."

"Which is why I was going to suggest an immediate visit to the Waifs and Strays Café," said Mr Perkins.

"The Waifs and Strays Café . . .?" echoed Rosie.

Henry struggled to explain. "It's a café for people who haven't got homes," he began.

"You mean for the homeless," said Rosie.

"Not exactly. The Waifs and Strays are people in training to become Homers!"

"This gets worse," said Rosie. "What, when pigs can fly, is a Homer?"

"Someone who makes people feel at home. Someone who turns unhappy houses into homes," said Henry.

"By releasing the Energy which is love," said Mr Perkins.

"By connecting the living and the dead," said Henry

"Ooh spook-ey!" said Rosie. They ignored her.

"By seeing people don't switch off," said Mr Perkins.

"I know a lot of switched-off people," said Rosie thoughtfully. "They've forgotten how to feel."

"Their Energy is blocked. They need Harvey Angell," said Mr Perkins, "to spark them into life, into love, into sonnets and odes, lyrics and laments, villanelles and . . ."

Mr Perkins was standing up on the log, waving his arms about.

"All right, all right. I get the picture," said Rosie. "So when are we going?"

"Going? Going?" said Mr Perkins, coming down from the log. (He'd been about to quote his favourite poet, Blake.)

"To this Waifs and Strays place," said Rosie.

"It's not that easy," said Henry. "You see you

56

can only find the café when Harvey Angell is with you."

"Great!" said Rosie. "So to find Harvey Angell we've got to find this café, but we can't find the café unless he's with us."

"That's about it," said Henry glumly.

"Unless," said Mr Perkins, "you have The Energy."

"Well, yes," said Henry, "unless some of Harvey Angell's Energy has rubbed off on you."

"And we have Sweetheart," said Mr Perkins.

"And Sweetheart's cosmic!" cried Rosie. "She's got cosmic energy!"

"Or Harvey Angell Energy," said Henry. "You mean we take Sweetheart with us?"

"It's worth a try," said Mr Perkins.

CHAPTER 9

Henry wrote the letter with Mr Perkins adding what he called 'asides' and Rosie correcting his spelling.

'Dear Harvey Angell,' wrote Henry. 'I am sorry to bother you but we need your help again.' ("Add 'urgently'," said Mr Perkins.)

'It is rather urgent,' Henry continued. 'I found a baby under the hollihocks.' ('Hollyhocks with a y,' said Rosie.)

'We think maybe you know about her. Lots of dark ladies keep coming to our house.' ("Witches," said Mr Perkins.)

'Mr Perkins thinks they are wiches,' wrote Henry. ("With a 't'," said Rosie.)

'Now the police have been and we are frightened Sweetheart – that's what we call her, because she is – will be taken away. Please, please help.

Love,
Henry xxx'

"P.S." said Rosie, "ASAP."

"P.P.S." said Mr Perkins. "If not sooner."

'P.P.P.S.' wrote Henry, when the others weren't looking. 'I miss you.'

They put the letter in an envelope addressed to Harvey Angell Esq. Rosie drew a picture in the corner of a rather funny looking Henry. Mr Perkins tucked the letter in his pocket.

They didn't tell the others where they were going.

"Don't want to get their hopes up," said Mr Perkins. "We'll just say we're going to the park."

But Aunt Agatha was anxious. "Mrs Sowerby's sure to be watching our every move," she said.

"Let her!" said Mr Perkins grandly. "What could look more natural and normal than taking Sweetheart to the park on a Sunday afternoon?"

"I suppose you're right," said Aunt Agatha doubtfully. "Be back for five. You're on the rota and we've two PWDs coming." Aunt Agatha consulted her growing collection of calling cards. "A Florence and a Lola. Five and five-thirty appointments," she said.

"We'll be back for Florence and Lola," Mr Perkins promised.

Aunt Agatha kissed Sweetheart goodbye. She'd learnt to do this like Sweetheart had learnt how to smile – by practice. The hollyhocks waved them off, jiggling and joggling as if in approval.

"It's not exactly a lie," said Henry as they pushed the pram down Ballantyre Road. "We do go past the park."

Mrs Sowerby was indeed watching. They saw her standing at an upstairs window.

"Wave!" instructed Mr Perkins. "And smile!"

"Perhaps she's lonely," said Rosie.

"Perhaps she's just nosey and nasty," said Henry.

"Now, now," said Mr Perkins. "Wave and smile."

They did both, if not very convincingly. Mrs Sowerby did neither.

Sweetheart, propped up in her pram with a pillow embroidered by Miss Muggins tucked behind her, seemed curiously excited. They kept the hood of the pram up so that passers-by couldn't see much of her, but it wasn't long before she began leaning forward and peering round the hood. Very soon her antennae popped out and she began clapping her hands and bleeping.

It was a bright, crisp afternoon. Snowdrops were out in the gardens. People were out washing their cars and chatting over garden fences.

The trio walked quickly. "Do you have any idea where this café is?" puffed Rosie whose legs were a good two inches shorter than Henry's.

"I know the general direction," said Henry. "If it's there. If we see it."

"Really helpful!" said Rosie.

Once beyond Ballantyre Road, Sweetheart's bleeps changed. Sometimes they were mild, contented sort of bleeps – almost as if she was singing to herself. But when they took a turning to the left, the bleeps suddenly became loud and alarmed.

"Do you think . . ." began Mr Perkins as they stopped at some traffic lights, "that Sweetheart . . ."

" . . . is directing us? Yes, oh yes!" shrieked Rosie and she leant into the pram to give Sweetheart a smacking kiss. "Brilliant cosmic babe!" cooed Rosie. "You're trying to tell us the way, aren't you?"

Sweetheart gave a single bleep. "I think that's a 'yes'," said Rosie. "Didn't I tell you? It's telepathy."

After that they just let Sweetheart lead the way through the Sunday-quiet town centre, on towards the river and the old cathedral.

"Do you remember, Henry, how we danced in the graveyard?" asked Mr Perkins.

"You in your pyjamas," said Henry, "and Mr Angell playing his flute."

"I was divinely sparked!" said Mr Perkins.

"In your pyjamas?" said Rosie.

"Yes, in my pyjamas," said Mr Perkins happily and he gave one of Rosie's plaits a tug. For once she didn't object.

On and on they walked. "I'm beginning to think this café doesn't exist," complained Rosie. "Or only in your dreams."

But at that moment Sweetheart's bleep reached a high-pitched frequency. They turned the corner and saw it. The Waifs and Strays

Café, gold moons and stars decorating the front, its interior hidden by the jungle of ferns and spider plants in the windows.

"Oh wow!" said Rosie, because standing on the pavement, directly outside the café, they could all feel a curious pull of energy tugging at them like a magnet does. Nervously, Mr Perkins smoothed down his few wisps of hair that were suddenly standing on end.

"It's up to you now, Henry," he said. "You've been here before."

Quite apart from the jangle of the café's door bell, it was impossible, with the pram and Sweetheart in it, to make a quiet entrance. An entrance which, it seemed, was only for Henry and Sweetheart. Mr Perkins and Rosie found themselves fixed in the doorway as if some invisible force stopped them moving any further.

Henry, with what he thought afterwards was his own flash of inspiration, said, "Hang on to the pram!" And as soon as they touched its handles, Mr Perkins and Rosie were released from whatever force had held them immobile and could move again. Into the café.

Inside, the café was divided into wooden booths. At first Rosie and Mr Perkins were too busy gazing up at the stars and moons on the ceiling, and the paintings of houses on the walls, to notice the faces peering round the sides of the wooden booths to look at them. But if they didn't notice the faces they couldn't fail to hear first a sudden silence and then a slow murmuring, building like the humming of bees.

"The child! The child! The child!" buzzed all round the café.

"I don't think I like this," whispered Mr Perkins.

"It's all right," said Henry, although his hands were shaking on the pram. "We're among friends." And as if in proof of this, Sweetheart smiled, waved her hands (and her antennae) and bowed left and right out of her pram for all the world like a queen in her carriage acknowledging her subjects.

As best he could, Henry scanned the room. He hadn't said so, but he'd been hoping they wouldn't need the letter, that they would find Harvey Angell here, waiting. But there was no sign of him.

Henry was glad when the waitress he remembered from his last visit came in from the kitchen at the back. The waitress's bright face broke into a smile. Henry smiled right back and then realised that the smile wasn't for him. Indeed the waitress wasn't even looking at him. She was all eyes, all smiles for Sweetheart.

"Well, isn't she a dindly, dandly dear!" said the waitress. One by one the customers of the Waifs and Strays Café emerged from their booths and gathered round the pram. Mr Perkins and Rosie found themselves backed up against a tall fern that tickled Mr Perkins' balding head and curled a few fond fronds round one of Rosie's plaits.

Henry, telling himself that everyone here *had* to be a friend of Harvey Angell's and that they were all either Homers or Homers-in-the-making, nevertheless held on tight to the pram's handle.

The café's customers were an extraordinary sight. Some, it's true, wore the kind of dungarees Harvey Angell wore, but others were dressed in bright Cossack trousers and boots. One or two wore jackets that looked as if they'd been woven out of rainbows. A woman, with hair down to her waist, wore a dress covered in sequins, another, a hat like a bowl of fruit. There were young men in silky striped boiler suits and one in top hat and tails. About all of them there was a sunny gentleness as if this was a welcoming party.

Not that anyone appeared to be welcoming Henry, Rosie and Mr Perkins. All eyes were on Sweetheart who promptly fell asleep as if just finding the café was enough for one day.

There was a general buzz of excitement. Comments whirled about Henry's head until he wanted to cry out, 'But what d'you mean? What d'you mean?'

"Heard she'd arrived."

"It was on the Fabulor."

"First time ever."

"Just slipped through they say."

"It was a crack, a crack somewhere."

"It won't be easy."

"Who's got the job?. Have you heard?

"What an advance, eh!"

Then one by one, as if it had all been pre-arranged, the café's customers departed. From nowhere, it seemed, each produced a flower and laid it on the pram until Sweetheart was sleeping under a blanket of flowers.

"Wait!" cried Henry. "Please wait! Please explain! We need help!"

But the strange customers only smiled and nodded at him. The woman in the sequined dress gave him a buttercup and said, "A blessing on you too, boy." Henry noticed that she tapped Rosie on the head with another buttercup and that sparks seemed to fly out of it. She did the same to Mr Perkins and he quivered all over as if he'd had a minor electric shock.

When the door had closed on the last of them, the waitress – who seemed to think it perfectly natural that all her customers should leave together – turned the sign on the café door to 'closed', and said, "There now, I should think you could all do with a drink of something."

They flopped at the nearest table. Mr Perkins mopped his brow with a non-too-clean hankie. Rosie scratched her head and made a few more sparks fly out.

"Here you are," said the waitress, reappearing with three tall glasses complete with straws. "Eternal Delight."

They drank. Sighed. Drank some more. Relaxed.

"I've met you before, haven't I?" said the waitress to Henry. "Forgotten your name, but I know what you ate."

"Supernova beefburgers," said Henry. "My name's Henry and I came here with Harvey Angell."

"Ah, that explains it," said the waitress. "You wouldn't have got in without one of us being with you and you wouldn't have got in today without her, the dindly dandly dear." The waitress nodded at Sweetheart.

"Please tell us what's going on," begged Henry. "Why did everyone leave like that?"

"They all seemed to know something about Sweetheart," said Rosie.

"But none of it made any sense," said Mr Perkins, "unless you count sparks coming out of people's heads and flowers coming out of nowhere, as sense. Which I don't," concluded Mr Perkins and he sucked up the last of his Eternal Delight and beamed round the table at everyone as if he no longer cared what made sense and what didn't. As if non-sense, like Eternal Delight, was much, much nicer.

CHAPTER 10

Tina, the waitress, untied her apron, fetched herself what looked like a very ordinary cup of tea and sat down at the table with them.

"The others," she said, "they had to go. You see none of them are assigned to you."

"Assigned?" queried Henry.

"Well, Harvey Angell was assigned to you, wasn't he?" said Tina.

"If you mean he came to our house and slept in the attic, then yes," said Henry.

"That's exactly what I mean," said Tina. "He was sent to you. It's against the rules for a Homer – or any of the trainees – to have contact with anyone they're not assigned to. Also this café is one of our special places. It's an ROE site."

"ROE?" Henry was even more puzzled.

"Renewal of Energy," said Tina. "A sort of re-charging of batteries. Forgive me saying so, but apart from this sweet babe here, you all have rather low Energy levels – and that affects everyone. More Eternal Delight?"

"Yes please," said Mr Perkins. "I think I've a poem coming on.

"Oh *please!*" said Henry. "Not now!"

"There's no stopping a poem," said Mr Perkins, "when it's on its way."

Tina grinned. (Her grin, Henry recognised, was the typical sunshiney Homer grin.) "I'd like to hear it," she said.

Mr Perkins immediately became shy. "Well, I've only got a few lines," he blustered. "It's still raw, if you know what I mean."

"Even so . . ." said Tina.

Henry and Rosie groaned. Mr Perkins stood up and recited:

> "I saw a dream in sequins,
> I heard a song of bliss
> I felt a touch upon my heart
> I thought it was a kiss."

Tina clapped.

"I hope you haven't forgotten you're in love with Aunt Agatha," said Henry, suddenly defensive on behalf of his Aunt.

"Of course not," said Mr Perkins, blushing.

"About Sweetheart," said Henry. "The people here, they seemed to know about her. It was almost as if she was expected."

But at this point Tina stood up and took away their glasses.

"I'm afraid I can't tell you anything," she said. "Against the rules, you see. We did have news that there's been a crack . . . a crack in . . ." But here Tina stopped, as if she'd already said more than she should.

"So you don't care that Sweetheart might be in danger?" Rosie burst out, turning red in the face.

"That's not fair," said Tina. "Of course I care about the dindly dandly dear. It's just that this isn't in my orbit."

"Orbit?" echoed Rosie.

"Within what I'm allowed to do," said Tina. "Or say. I'd like to help you but I can't."

"We've got a letter here for Harvey Angell," said Mr Perkins, producing it from his pocket.

"Ah well, that's a different matter," said Tina.

"Will you give it him?" they asked, as one.

"Course I will," said Tina. "If I see him."

"IF?" cried Henry.

"Well, he's not a regular you know," said Tina. "And he could be working anywhere. He comes in when he can."

All three of them looked so cast down at this, that Tina took pity on them. "Look, I'll try to get a message to him on the Fabulor," she said. "That's our kind of e-mail. And rather more efficient than yours."

Mr Perkins handed over the letter. Tina tucked it behind the Eternal Delight machine. She gave them each a rather tingly kiss goodbye. They left the café feeling anxious but hopeful.

"Harvey Angell won't let us down," said Mr Perkins. "After all it was him who sent Sweetheart to us."

"We don't know that for sure," said Henry. "And anyway, Harvey Angell doesn't think about time like we do. His 'now' isn't like our 'now.' If he turned up in six weeks he'd still think that was 'now'."

But Rosie and Mr Perkins were more optimistic. Henry wasn't sure if it was real optimism or just the effect of the café and the glasses of Eternal Delight. He could tell by the dreamy look in Mr Perkins's eyes that he was what they'd come to know as 'Lost in Poem'. As for Rosie, who had trudged the last mile to the café, complaining all the way, she was now skipping along so quickly that they had a hard job keeping up with her. One or two last, lingering sparks flew from her hair.

Henry sighed. Neither the café nor the drink of Eternal Delight seemed to have had the same effect on him. He looked at Sweetheart and wanted to lift her from her pram and hold her close and safe for ever and ever. Loving someone, thought Henry, made your heart grow larger. And it made it ache. Henry's ached some more when they got back to Ballantyre Road – late – and there were Florence and Lola, together and waiting, and there was Mrs Sowerby, up in her window, watching. Watching grimly.

Florence and Lola sat on the garden wall, their faces as long as their black skirts. They looked worn thin with sorrow.

"Were they *ever* young and happy?" asked Mr

Perkins, but this seemed so impossible to imagine that neither Henry nor Rosie bothered to answer.

"They look as if something so awful has happened to them that they can never forget it," said Rosie. As they approached 131, Florence and Lola stood up. A look of hope and eagerness flashed over both faces. Lola, the younger of the two, started forward. Florence followed, hugging her arms about herself as if she feared falling apart.

Both women gazed into the pram. Sweetheart opened her eyes and smiled. At once Florence and Lola burst into tears.

It always happened. All the Poor Witchy Dears looked at Sweetheart and wept. This time, perhaps because he so feared losing Sweetheart, Henry found the tears coming to his own eyes and had to brush them away.

"Can I hold her?" asked Florence in that strange echoey voice the women shared.

She was not the first to ask and they always said no. It had been agreed that it was far too risky. Aunt Agatha still refused to believe either in witches or magic spells, but as Miss Skivvy said, 'better safe than sorry.'

Henry had other things to worry about apart from spells. Right now PC 45 and PC 16 and the mention of Social Services. Social Services might not deal in spells, but Henry knew they had power. Power to take Sweetheart away.

Florence and Lola trailed down the road, their arms about each other. Inconsolable.

★　★　★

Henry had trouble sleeping that night. It was his turn to have Sweetheart in his room. She had grown out of the drawer-cradle and slept in a cot they'd bought from Rosie's mum who'd kept Rosie's own cot for years and years – 'just in case'.

Growing out of the drawer-cradle wasn't the only change in Sweetheart. Some of them were the ordinary, expected kind of changes – though in Sweetheart's case these seemed to happen faster than usual. She could sit up and had grown lots more hair. She could drink her vegetable juice from a cup with a spout.

But there were other, stranger changes. Changes that were hard to define. For instance, to judge by Sweetheart's bleeps (fast and high when something was about to happen, or someone about to arrive), she knew when the postman was coming before any of them could see him. Once she had seen and waved at Rosie from right across the other side of the park and yards and yards before Henry had seen her.

Only yesterday, Miss Muggins had said, "I think Sweetheart knows what I'm thinking. If I'm a bit sad she pats my hand and makes a kind of kissing noise."

Henry and Rosie had exchanged looks.

Neither of them had said anything, but both had the identical thought – telepathic powers.

Sweetheart's 'powers' excited Rosie and worried Henry. Rosie thought of all the things Sweetheart would be able to do. "She'll see buses coming from miles away," said Rosie, "and when she's at school she'll know exactly what the teacher's thinking. And when it comes to exams she'll know the questions in advance."

But Henry thought of the Mrs Sowerbys of this world who would consider Sweetheart an alien, who would call the police, who would want Sweetheart put 'in care'. Seeing buses miles away and knowing what your teacher thought, couldn't compensate for that, Henry thought. And it was odd how children were only put 'in care' when they didn't have anyone of their own to care for them properly.

"But you do, don't you, Little Sis?" said Henry to Sweetheart.

Sweetheart had no problem sleeping. She lay on her back showing her belly button, her hands up by her ears. Quite obviously her telepathic powers didn't work while she slept or she would have known that Henry was tossing and turning.

He slept in snatches. The same questions went round and round in his head. *Had* Harvey Angell sent Sweetheart to them? Would he get the letter? And if he got the letter, would he come? And when?

Once, during a snatch of sleep, Henry dreamt that Lola, like the thirteenth fairy at the christening, had put a spell on Sweetheart so that she would sleep for a hundred years. He woke Sweetheart up just to make sure it *was* a dream. Sweetheart gave him a smile as if to say, 'silly!' and went back to sleep.

Henry plumped his pillow, turned over on his left side and tried remembering Mr Perkins' poems. But now all the brightly dressed figures from the Waifs and Strays Café flitted in and out of his dreams and he kept hearing their words – 'just slipped through . . .' 'it was a crack, a crack somewhere', then he would wake with a start as if there'd been a crack in his dream.

It felt as if it was still the middle of the night and that he hadn't slept at all when he woke to hear what sounded like the distant roar of a dragon. A silence and then the roar again.

Henry checked Sweetheart. She was wide awake already, her antennae out, her smile on, her bleep off. Sweetheart looked as if she was listening in, not to a dragon's roar, but to some wonderful, some heavenly music.

Henry ran to the attic window and pulled back the curtains. It was almost dawn. The houses in the street that ran behind Ballantyre Road were still in darkness. One or two birds were just beginning to sound the morning out. A tree was turning from black to greeney-grey.

But Henry didn't notice any of this because what he saw, framed in the window, hanging in the sky and drifting gently downwards was the great puffed-up pear of a hot-air balloon, sky blue and floating directly above the back garden.

Henry flung open the window and leant out. The roar he'd heard had been from the fire beneath the balloon's basket which, as the balloon descended, went out. And now Henry could see the man, hauling on the ropes of the big blue pear. Then the basket bounced on the ground several times. The body of the balloon collapsed and lay across the lawn like the skin of some fabulously rare animal, and a man hopped cheerfully out of the basket. A man with a thatch of yellow hair. A man wearing bright knee patches on his dungarees.

"Morning, Henry!" said Harvey Angell. "Any chance of breakfast?"

CHAPTER 11

It was the breakfast of breakfasts. Aunt Agatha burst out of meanness and into abundance like a rose going from bud to bloom.

Henry had woken everyone up, rushing from room to room shouting, "He's here! Harvey Angell's here!" And now they were all gathered in the kitchen in slippers and dressing gowns, PJs and nighties. Harvey Angell sat in the rocking chair with Sweetheart in his arms. He had kissed her nose, her tummy and all ten of her toes. Sweetheart cooed, gurgled and bleeped.

Aunt Agatha cooked bacon and eggs, sausages, tomatoes and mushrooms. Mr Perkins made toast. Miss Skivvy found honey. Miss Muggins made tea. They were all of a scuttle. They were almost, thought Henry, a family.

And as this was going on, a small figure with ginger plaits appeared at the back door.

"I saw the balloon," said Rosie gazing at Harvey Angell and suddenly turning shy.

"This is Rosie," said Henry. "She's helped us a lot."

Harvey Angell gave Rosie his 500 kilowatt beam. Rosie, immediately smitten, found a stool and sat as near to Harvey Angell as she could without getting in the way of the breakfast makers.

"I know the rhyme," she whispered. "Your rhyme. Henry taught me."

It was the cue for them all to join in. Harvey Angell bounced Sweetheart on his knee while they sang:

> "Watts and volts
> Watts and volts
> Better by far
> Than thunderbolts."

The bacon sizzled and the toast toasted and Miss Muggins put a big pot of tea on the table.

Harvey Angell beamed at them all and turned to Rosie. "I can see at once that you're a natural mother," he said. Rosie turned the colour of her name and pretended to be busy tickling Sweetheart's toes.

Aunt Agatha's generosity did not extend to giving everyone bacon, sausages, eggs etcetera. But Mr Perkins had toasted almost an entire loaf of bread, the pot of honey was new, the pot of tea large and very soon they were all tucking in while Sweetheart was passed from knee to knee and offered an occasional honeyed finger to lick.

"We've looked after her for you," said Mr Perkins between crunches of toast.

"And it's been a pleasure," said Miss Muggins.

"Despite the Poor Witchy Dears," said Miss Skivvy.

"And the expense," said Aunt Agatha.

Harvey Angell put down his knife and fork. "Hold on a minute," he said. "Did you say you'd looked after her *for me?*"

"It *had* to be you," said Mr Perkins. "Henry found her under the hollyhocks. We think of the hollyhocks as . . ." Mr Perkins struggled to explain himself.

"As yours," said Miss Skivvy.

"In the know," said Miss Muggins.

"Magical," said Henry.

"Well," said Harvey Angell, helping himself to toast and honey, "I admit to having a certain influence over the hollyhocks; to being in tune with them, you might say. As for Sweetheart, well I'd heard – the way we Homers *do* hear of all matters relating to time – that a child had slipped through. But until I had your letter, I had no idea she'd come to you."

All round the table faces fell.

"But if it wasn't you . . .?" began Mr Perkins, instantly losing his appetite for toast.

"Then we don't know *where* she's come from," said Aunt Agatha whisking away Harvey Angell's plate as if she now regretted filling it so full.

Henry said nothing. It was as if everything

Harvey Angell had said had washed through his head, everything but one phrase. One phrase that his mind now repeated to itself over and over again. "A CHILD HAD SLIPPED THROUGH. A CHILD HAD SLIPPED THROUGH." And Henry heard again the confusing voices of the café. 'Just slipped through.' 'A crack, a crack somewhere.' 'First in ages.'

The remembered voices crowded out everything but one thought. If Sweetheart had 'slipped through' (though *through what* Henry couldn't imagine), what was to stop her *slipping away*? And he looked at Sweetheart sitting on Rosie's lap, tugging at one of Rosie's plaits and thought, 'I can't bear it. I can't bear it!'

Then he came round to see Harvey Angell smiling directly at him and the thought, like a soapy bubble, popped and vanished.

"Cheer up," Harvey Angell said to everyone at the table. "Things aren't as bad as you think. I can tell you what I know about Sweetheart . . ."

"What?" demanded six voices.

Harvey Angell took another cup of tea and leant back in his chair.

"We'd heard there was a child," he said, "who'd slipped through a crack in time . . ."

"A crack in time!" echoed Miss Muggins, her eyes wide with fright as though a crack in time might equal a crack in the ground through which she might fall with a great PLOP.

"It has happened before," continued Harvey Angell, "but not for many centuries."

"But *how* does it happen?" asked Henry.

"Quite easily, really," said Harvey Angell. "And quite naturally. Have you ever seen a shaft of sunlight on a hillside? Or a finger of light stretching from the sky to the surface of a lake?"

They all nodded. They had.

"Well, it's like that," said Harvey Angell. "Only much more intense, of course. The light becomes like the blade of a knife. A knife that cuts through time."

"And someone slips through it," said Mr Perkins. "How very poetic."

"It sounds like someone going down a slide in the park," said Rosie. "When they don't mean to."

"And they get themselves to the bottom and find themselves in a different century," said Henry.

"I'd love a go!" said Mr Perkins.

"And they've slipped forwards a hundred years," said Miss Skivvy with the air of one solving a major scientific problem.

"It is something like that," said Harvey Angell. "Only Sweetheart hasn't slipped forwards in time. She's slipped backwards."

There was a long silence while they all took this in. Sweetheart went off into a long, happy bleeping as though at last someone really understood her.

"You mean," said Henry slowly, "that Sweetheart's come from the future."

"Got it in one, Henry," said Harvey Angell.

"And the next question is from how far forward in the future has she come?"

"Does she have to go back – I mean forward?" asked Henry in a very small voice.

"I'm afraid she does," said Harvey Angell. "And it's not going to be easy."

CHAPTER 12

There and then Harvey Angell set up his Connecting Kit on the kitchen table. Henry smiled to see the Energy Charger and Century Clock again, remembering how he had sneaked up to the attic to spy on Harvey Angell's mysterious gear. How puzzled he'd been then by the Clock, its face so covered in flowers and animals that you could hardly see the numbers. He'd been even more puzzled by the numbers. Instead of going one to twelve, like the kitchen clock, these numbers went from eleven to twenty-four. They represented, Henry'd discovered, not hours but centuries.

On the first visit to Ballantyre Road, Harvey Angell had set the clock at nineteen for the nineteenth century. For 1898, in fact, the year Henry's Great Grandma Ellie was born. 'Every house has a presiding spirit,' Harvey Angell had said. And back then, when Aunt Agatha had been withering and the whole house freighted with gloom, 'the presiding spirit' had been that of Great Grandma Ellie.

Now, without a doubt, it was Sweetheart.

They gathered round the kitchen table to watch as Harvey Angell attached the Energy Charger to a socket at the back of the Clock. Immediately the red finger of the charger leapt like a startled rabbit and the Clock began to tick and tock, slowly, as if it was struggling with time itself and finding it too heavy.

Very delicately Harvey Angell moved the Clock's single silver fuse-wire finger from nineteen to twenty. From twenty to twenty-one. From twenty-one to twenty-two. They were all holding their breath. Then the finger touched twenty-three and suddenly the Clock seemed to come alive. The Charger's red finger zoomed to 'Full On'. The Clock's tick and tock became brisk and regular as if it was now confident of itself and its purpose and Sweetheart, sitting up in her newly acquired high chair, smiled and clapped her hands.

"There!" said Harvey Angell, standing back and looking very pleased with himself. "I'd say that was about the year 2230 – maybe 2235."

There was a stunned silence in the kitchen.

"You mean," said Henry in a voice that quivered at the edges, "Sweetheart's slipped through from – from the twenty-third century?"

"Give or take a few years," said Harvey Angell cheerfully. "Amazing, isn't it?"

It struck Henry as both amazing and awful. "But she's way out of her time!" he cried.

"Not as unusual as you'd think," said Harvey

Angell, packing away the Clock and Charger. "I've met lots of people living in the twenty-first century who would be more at home in the sixteenth."

"Yes," mused Mr Perkins. "I'd be more at home in the nineteenth century. Walking with Wordsworth, browsing with Blake . . ."

"Perkins. Please concentrate on the present," said Aunt Agatha sharply.

"And perhaps the future," said Harvey Angell.

"Told you," said Rosie, nudging Henry in the ribs. "Sweetheart's the child of the future."

"Yes," said Harvey Angell, "Rosie's right. In Sweetheart we can see how the human race will evolve."

Rosie smirked.

"You mean we're all going to have antennae," squeaked Miss Muggins, "and bleep and have buttercup ears?"

"Sweetheart's antennae, as you call them, are probably very valuable sensors enabling her to pick up the electrical brain waves of others. Elephant trunk fish can do it already, you know," said Harvey Angell.

"Good for elephant trunk fish," muttered Aunt Agatha.

"Told you so," said Rosie, giving Henry another nudge. "Telepathy." (Rosie was getting altogether too smug, thought Henry.)

"As for the bleeps," continued Harvey Angell, "my guess is that she has some kind of genetically induced computer system inside her. Save

84

her carrying a lap-top about the place. Probably needs connecting."

"But won't she talk?" asked Henry suddenly thinking how lonely Sweetheart was going to be if she *couldn't* talk.

"For that I'm afraid she needs to be in her own time. And probably with her mother," Harvey Angell answered.

It was Aunt Agatha who asked the question none of them really wanted answering. "Now that we know she's from the twenty-third century, how do we get her back there?"

"With luck – a great deal of luck," said Harvey Angell, "her mother will come for her."

"Slipping through . . ." said Henry.

"Which is far from easy," said Harvey Angell. "So we need a plan in case she doesn't make it. The Clock's told us the century Sweetheart's come from – the 'When' if you like. What we need to know now is the 'Where'. *Where* in the twenty-third century?"

And then Miss Skivvy made the suggestion that made them all feel deeply alarmed. "What if one of the Poor Witchy Dears is Sweetheart's mother?" she said.

"No!" said Henry, almost rivalling Aunt Agatha by looking so fierce. "Even if that was true, I'd never let Sweetheart go to one of the Poor Witchy Dears. She'd forget how to smile."

"She'd wear a black bonnet," said Miss Skivvy thoughtfully.

"I don't want to think about it," said Henry.

"You don't need to worry," said Harvey Angell. "The Poor Witchy Dears as you call them, are ghost mothers. The Mothers of Lamentation."

It made them all shiver when Harvey Angell said this and when he explained that the women, in their black clothes, were mothers who had lost a child. "Mothers who without another child to comfort them, never stop lamenting and grieving."

It was enough to start Miss Muggins doing both. She wept into her tea. "We should never have called them witches," she sobbed. "How very unkind."

"You weren't to know," Harvey Angell said, putting his arm round her, "and anyway, grief is like a kind of fog that seeps under the door and through the windows and makes everything grey. I expect you felt like that."

"I did, I did," said Miss Muggins drying her eyes on the sleeve of her cardigan.

The odd thing was that although several of the Mothers of Lamentation, the Ghost Mothers (as they were now careful to call them) had appointments, none of them turned up.

"On holiday," Mr Perkins suggested flippantly. But Henry thought it was the presence of Harvey Angell that kept them away.

Whichever theory was right, they all felt as relieved as if a dark shadow had been lifted from their lives. They stopped dreading the knock on the door. They abandoned the rota. Apart from his Connecting Kit and his 500 kilowatt beam, Harvey Angell brought with him something they all badly needed. Hope.

For Henry there were two hopes – two hopes at war with each other. He wanted Sweetheart to be happy and, at heart, he knew that meant Sweetheart being with her mother again. (That was Hope One.) And he wanted Sweetheart to stay at Ballantyre Road for ever and ever. (That was Hope Two.) But all of them – even the usually doubting Aunt Agatha – felt sure that Harvey Angell would sort everything out. Why, Harvey Angell had even managed to transform Mrs Sowerby. So what *couldn't* he do?

Mrs Sowerby appeared on the doorstep soon after Harvey Angell's arrival.

"Now it's men in balloons!" she said, glowering at Mr Perkins. "More aliens, I suppose. I'm not the only one, you know. I've witnesses in the street who saw him arrive, and you can be sure I'll be reporting . . ."

"Mrs Sowerby!" said Harvey Angell, appearing alongside Mr Perkins at the door. "How exceptionally nice to meet you. I've heard what a watchful neighbour you are. And we all need someone to watch over us, don't we? Won't you come in?"

Mrs Sowerby looked first doubtful, then dazed. Harvey Angell gave her the full 500 kilowatt beam.

("She melted," Mr Perkins said later, "simply melted!")

Mrs Sowerby followed Harvey Angell into the kitchen like a Mini towed by a Mercedes. Once there, Harvey Angell insisted she take the rocking chair ('much the most comfy'), called on Henry to supply cushions, Miss Skivvy to make fresh tea, and Mr Perkins to bring a stool because clearly Mrs Sowerby needed to put her feet up for a while. And when all this was accomplished, Harvey Angell did the most unexpected thing of all. He picked up Sweetheart and deposited her in Mrs Sowerby's lap.

"You won't mind holding her for a minute, will you?" he said. And Sweetheart sat there giving her very best smile and patting Mrs Sowerby's cheek.

To Henry's astonishment, he saw Mrs Sowerby was crying and smiling both together.

"If ever we're in need of a baby sitter, I'm sure we can call on you," said Harvey Angell. At which Rosie looked distinctly put out.

* * *

"So that was Mrs Sowerby sorted," said Mr Perkins later.

"And the Ghost Mothers have gone," said Henry.

"For the time being," said Aunt Agatha.

But Harvey Angell had other things on his mind. "I need to get back to the Waifs and Strays Café," he said. "One of the elders keeps a Missing-Persons-in-Time list. If Sweetheart is on it, we might learn not just when-in-time she's from, but where."

"I don't see that knowing 'where' makes much difference," said Miss Skivvy.

"It's obvious," said Rosie. "If Sweetheart came from America, then her mother might thinks she's there. She might 'slip through' into America and be searching everywhere."

All this went out of everyone's mind because before Harvey Angell could get back from the Waifs and Strays Café with any news, the question, 'where has Sweetheart come *from*?' had changed to 'where has Sweetheart *gone*?'

CHAPTER 13

It happened when Rosie was allowed to take Sweetheart to the park on her own. They all wanted to go back to the Waifs and Strays Café but Harvey Angell said only Henry could come. "It disturbs the Energy levels too much," he said, "and Gabriel wouldn't be pleased." Gabriel was the Elder who kept the Missing-Persons-in-Time list.

Only Rosie sulked. Miss Muggins said she was going to knit Sweetheart another cardigan. Mr Perkins said he had a poem on the go about balloons in eternity. Aunt Agatha said the kitchen cupboard was bare, she must shop. Miss Skivvy was secretly planning a nice little siesta, drifting off to a radio play, maybe.

To keep Rosie happy, Aunt Agatha said she could take Sweetheart to the park.

"Can I sit with her on the swings?" asked Rosie.

"Provided you promise to keep tight hold of her," said Aunt Agatha, "and make sure no-one else is around. We don't want anyone else reporting us to the police."

Rosie promised. It was a rather drizzly afternoon but Rosie dressed Sweetheart in her best bonnet and the woolly coat Miss Muggins had knitted. She tucked Sweetheart in the pram and set forth.

Rosie felt very important walking down Ballantyre Road by herself, pushing the pram as if she was, at the very least, Sweetheart's big sister, possibly her mother. She wished she was just a little bit taller or the pram smaller because the handle came almost to her chin making it difficult to look as grand as she wished to look. All the same, she felt very professional, with a bottle (of cabbage juice) and Sweetheart's beaker tucked under the blanket should Sweetheart become thirsty, and a spare nappy. Just in case.

On the way to the park Rosie sang all the songs she thought Sweetheart might like. She sang, 'I Had a Little Nut Tree', 'Three Blind Mice' and 'Pop Goes the Weasel'. Sweetheart didn't bleep. She made a noise that sounded, to Rosie, like 'La la la. La la la.' Rosie thought that when she grew up she would have six babies of her own, three boys and three girls and they would all be very happy and very clean and very good. Much like Sweetheart.

Rosie wished she could lower Sweetheart's hood and so encourage people to stop and admire her, but it was still raining and anyway she didn't dare.

The rain had obviously kept the children away because the park was quiet, the swings and slides neglected. "Well, at least we can have a little fun," Rosie said to Sweetheart and she lifted her from the pram, dried the seat of the swing with her hankie and sat down with Sweetheart in her lap. Rosie used her feet to get them going then swung gently to and fro, singing a swinging song.

Sweetheart loved it. Rosie sang:

"How do you like to go up in a swing,
Up in the air so blue?
O I do think its the pleasantest thing
Ever a child can do!"

And Sweetheart bleeped and went "La la la," as if she agreed with every word of this. As if in answer to the song, the sky began to clear and show blue. The sun struggled out. The grass shone with a new, fresh green. Very tiny buds were appearing on the huge horse-chestnut trees like a promise of spring.

Sweetheart began bleeping. Her bleeps became faster and faster, higher and higher in pitch. Rosie should have been warned, but she wasn't. She thought Sweetheart was just excited by the swing. She didn't even see the Ghost Mother drifting towards them on feet that scarcely seemed to touch the ground, her black dress brushing the grass.

It was as if the sky had suddenly closed off its blueness. The Ghost Mother stood before them holding out her arms to Sweetheart. Rosie

92

stopped the swing with a jerk. The Ghost Mother smiled. She wasn't one of the women Rosie had seen before. This one, although almost transparently thin, was young and quite pretty. She had blue eyes and hair the colour of the palest primroses.

"What a Sweetheart!" said the Ghost Mother and Rosie saw the tears coming into her eyes. Perhaps because the Ghost Mother, unknowingly, had called Sweetheart by her name, or perhaps because of what Harvey Angell had said about the Mothers of Lamentation, or perhaps for both reasons, Rosie suddenly felt an overwhelming pang of sorrow for the young Ghost Mother.

Rosie thought of her own mother and how badly she had wanted more children. How perfectly awful it would have been if she, Rosie, had died. Rosie felt sure her mother would have gone on looking for her for ever and ever. The thought made the tears come to her own eyes.

So when the Ghost Mother asked – as all the Ghost Mothers had asked, time after time – "Can I hold her?" – Rosie thought, well why not? What harm could there be in it? "Just for a moment," she said, and slipping off the swing she passed Sweetheart into the Ghost Mother's arms.

They were gone in an instant. Without a sound. If Sweetheart bleeped it was at a pitch too high for Rosie to hear. In shock, she looked about her disbelievingly. Perhaps she'd blinked.

Perhaps Sweetheart was miraculously back in her pram? (She wasn't.) Perhaps if she climbed to the top step of the slide, she would see them, running across the park, could give chase, could rescue Sweetheart.

But there was no sign of them. No black figure. No small baby. Sweetheart and the Ghost Mother had vanished. Vanished into thin air.

* * *

In the Waifs and Strays Café, Henry and Harvey Angell sat opposite Gabriel. Gabriel might have been a farmer or someone who'd worked in the fields all his life. His face was kindly, weather-beaten, wise and nearly as old as the book he had in front of him on the table. He had a way of tilting his head to one side and listening very carefully. He had listened carefully to Henry's account of finding Sweetheart under the holly-hocks and to Harvey Angell's 'reading' of the Century Clock. Henry tried to read the names in the book upside down. He could see that under the column labelled 'lost and found', there were very few ticks indicating found.

"Of course most people are lost in the past," said Gabriel, turning the rather tattered and ink spattered pages of the book.

"How do you hear about them?" asked Henry.

"That's easy," answered Gabriel. "As you know, we Homers work in all time. Though when it comes to the future, we have our problems." For a moment Gabriel's cheery face looked sombre. "We get reports, see. From all over time and place. Here's William Doddington, lost in the 18th century, found in the 16th. But I'm afraid there's nothing here about your Sweetheart."

"Do you get reports from the future too?" asked Henry.

"That's not what I was looking for," said Gabriel. "I was looking at reports from Homers in other countries. See if one of them had spotted a mother who had slipped through into the present time and was looking for her child. There's been no sightings." Gabriel closed the book with a sigh.

"So what do we do next?" asked Henry.

"The best we can hope for is that Sweetheart's mother is still trying to slip through. That she still might make it," said Gabriel.

"And the worst?" asked Henry, because both Gabriel and Harvey Angell were now looking seriously anxious.

"The thing is," said Gabriel reluctantly, "that although all time is one, none of us can survive for long outside the time we truly belong to."

"What about William Doddington?" demanded Henry, "He seemed to do all right slipping from the 18th to the 16th century."

"Ah, that one was never at home in the 18th," said Gabriel, "so he was perfectly fine in the 16th. But Sweetheart's different. I can tell you've looked after her wonderfully well, but in part she's been living off her first days of mother-love."

"And now that's running out, isn't it?" said Henry. A rising panic made him go tense all over. "That's what you're trying to tell me. That unless Sweetheart's mother comes soon she might . . ." He couldn't finish the sentence.

"Hold on, hold on," chided Gabriel. "It's true we need Sweetheart's mother to come soon – let's say within the next week or two. But if she doesn't we're going to have to think of other ways of returning her."

"Other ways? *What* other ways?" Henry could hardly keep still on his chair.

"It's very difficult," said Harvey Angell, "but I could take her."

"Not only difficult but dangerous," said Gabriel. He and Harvey Angell exchanged one of those looks grown-ups sometimes share when something so awful has happened, or is about to happen, that it can't be spoken of in front of the children.

"Why dangerous?" asked Henry for now he was imagining Sweetheart lost in space, unable to go backwards or forwards in time and blee-ping sadly to herself.

"That's not your problem, Henry," said Harvey Angell, slapping him on the shoulder. "It's mine."

And Henry, who couldn't bear to think about – let alone hear about – any danger that Sweetheart might face, asked no further questions.

He slipped his hand inside Harvey Angell's and hoped. Harvey Angell, thought Henry, had magic enough to cope with anything. If anyone could beat time, past, present *or* future, it was Harvey Angell. Wasn't it?

CHAPTER 14

Pushing the empty pram back to Ballantyre Road was the hardest thing Rosie had ever done. She could hardly put one foot in front of the other. The pram, which should have felt lighter, felt heavier. Heavy with guilt and fear. Rosie didn't know how she could face anyone, least of all Henry. Tears ran down her cheeks as she walked. Several women stopped to ask if she was all right but Rosie just shook her head and kept going.

Then what she dreaded, happened. They met in the street; Henry and Harvey Angell returning from the Waifs and Strays Café and Rosie, pale-faced and weeping, pushing her lonely load back from the park.

Henry ran towards her. "Rosie! What is it? What's the matter?" he cried.

There was no need for an answer. The empty pram was evidence enough. "Where is she?" Henry demanded. "Where's Sweetheart? What have you done with her?" Shaking himself, he was ready to shake an answer out of Rosie.

"Let her speak," said Harvey Angell, catching up with them.

And in between sobs Rosie said, "The G-g-g-host Mother. She wanted to hold Sweetheart . . ."

"You know we agreed never to let any of them do that," shouted Henry.

"I kn-kn-kn-know," wailed Rosie. "But I was s-s-sorry for her. And I thought it would be all right. Just for a moment. Then they vanished. B-b-both of them. Just vanished!" And abandoning the pram, Rosie sat down on the pavement's edge, buried her face in her knees and howled.

Henry turned to Harvey Angell. "We've got to find her," he said. "We've got to!"

But Harvey Angell was already rushing into the house, stripping off his shirt and dungarees as he went. "I know!" he shouted. "And I'm off. Now!"

"But where? Where?" cried Henry. "Can I come?"

"Absolutely not," said Harvey Angell disappearing into the sitting room which had been turned into a bedroom for him. "I'm going to the City of Shadows."

In no time at all, Harvey Angell had changed into a sky-blue boiler suit, the logo of earth stamped on the front pocket. He'd strange silver trainers on his feet and a bright Rasta hat on his thatch.

They waited for him in the kitchen. The

kitchen that in just a few minutes had become like a funeral parlour with Sweetheart's empty pram and empty high chair like mournful reminders of her absence. Rosie had cried so much that now she had hiccups. Miss Muggins was snuggling one of Sweetheart's blankets. Aunt Agatha and Mr Perkins held hands. Henry stood at the window frozen, like a statue. Rosie sobbed and hiccupped in the rocking chair.

Harvey Angell said nothing until he had set up the Connecting Kit again. This time he attached a small time-wave cassette recorder. That done he took three deep breaths. No-one had ever seen him looking so grim.

"Round the table everyone," he ordered and they all gathered.

"For Sweetheart and I to get back," he said, "I need you all to keep in contact with this." He pointed to the time-wave cassette. "One or other of you must keep talking, singing, whatever you like, only keep it going. All night if necessary. I'll have my receiver." He took from his pocket what looked like the most miniature mobile phone any of them had seen. "I'll be able to tune in whenever necessary. Is that understood?"

They all nodded silently. None of them dared ask *when* it might be necessary. Or why.

"One last thing," said Harvey Angell, "keep your spirits up!" He flashed them a quick, last 500 kilowatt beam and was gone, taking with him only the tiny receiver and his flute.

Watching him go, Henry saw the hollyhocks which had become their usual bright selves, darken and shudder.

* * *

In the centre of the City of Shadows, home of the Ghost Mothers, is the Lake of Tears. To reach it is usually a three day journey through rivers of mud and hills of slime. But for Harvey Angell's slime-proof, mud-proof, silver trainers, he would never have made it.

Nor without his flute and the voices of Henry and Co. would he have made it through the forests of black poplars and sterile willows that oozed sadness like eucalyptus oozes gum. And nor without his sky-blue boiler suit and bright Rasta cap would he have survived the swamps and the fierce biting Doubts that swarmed about him like midges on a hot day.

Even with all this, even with the extra Energy that all Homers possess, it is impossible to reach the City of Shadows without being overtaken by feelings of despair and hopelessness. It is the lack of colour, of seasons, of growing things, of a glimpse of blue sky.

Often on his journey, Harvey Angell had to stop and sit on a rotting stump and tune in to Ballantyre Road.

They kept it going. Harvey Angell listened to Mr Perkins reading poems. Mr Perkins read limericks and comic verse. He made Harvey

Angell laugh with 'The Owl and the Pussy Cat'. He read:

' "Will you walk a little faster?" said a whiting
to a snail,
"There's a porpoise close behind me and he's
treading on my tail." '

Mr Perkins made up limericks about young ladies from Gwent, Chester, Norwich, and Penzance.

Aunt Agatha played the piano and the others all sang. They sang 'One potato, two potato'. They made up a version of 'Ten Green Bottles' that reached as far as sixty-six green bottles.

Harvey Angell would listen for five minutes or so and then, with his spirits lifted, head on for the City of Shadows and the Lake of Tears.

At the entrance to the City were Watch-Birds, sharp eyed and beaked. Harvey Angell sat on the ground and played his flute until one after the other the birds tipped upside down like bats do, dangled by their feet and slept.

At this point Harvey Angell had to tune in again to Ballantyre Road where, although by now it was the middle of the night, Henry was telling all the jokes he had ever heard. (It was clear from his voice that he was having a hard time finding them funny.)

Once past the Watch-Birds there was only the Ancient Mother to deal with. The Ancient Mother sat at an old treadle sewing machine stitching black gowns. She herself was all in grey apart from her black-booted feet working the treadle. About her were rolls of black cloths. Cottons, taffetas and silks made inky pools on the ground at her feet. Newly made dresses hung like shrouds from the branches of dead trees.

Harvey Angell hid. He closed his eyes and summoned up every drop of Energy he possessed and then he stepped in front of the Ancient Mother, his sky-blue suit so dazzling that she had to cover her eyes.

In that moment he rushed past her, brushing aside the dangling black robes that seemed to want to cling to him. And there, at the end of a stoney path lined with brambles and tall nettles that tore at his suit and stung his face, was the Lake of Tears.

And there were the Ghost Mothers sitting in a circle on the banks of the Lake and passing Sweetheart round the circle as if this was some awful version of Pass the Parcel. They held Sweetheart under her arms and as they passed her from one Mother to the next, they chanted:

"One-ery, two-ery, tickery, seven,
Hallibo, crackibo, ten and eleven,
Spin, span, muskidan,
Twiddle-um, twaddle-um, twenty-one."

As Harvey Angell listened and watched, hidden behind a withered bush, they began a new and alarming game. Sweetheart, wrapped in a black shawl, was put in a basket and the basket put in the crook of a tree. One Ghost

Mother rocked it. One bent the branch. One caught Sweetheart as she fell. All of them sang:

"Rock a bye baby
In the tree tops
When the bough breaks
The cradle will fall."

There was only one thing Harvey Angell could do. He began playing his flute.

The Ghost Mothers were not as easy to charm as the Watch-Birds had been. But the tune Harvey Angell played was full of memories. Each Ghost Mother, remembering her own lost child, lay down on the bank and slept. As Harvey Angell crept nearer, still playing, he could see that each of the Ghost Mothers wore a small contented smile.

Harvey Angell grabbed Sweetheart from the basket, tossed aside the black shawl, unzipped his boiler suit and tucked Sweetheart inside it so that just her eyes, nose and one antennae peeped out. Then he began making his way back. Back down the stoney path, protecting Sweetheart from the brambles and nettles. Back past the Ancient Mother, snoring on her stool – for the sound of the flute had reached her too. Back past the Watch-Birds now just beginning to wake and right themselves on their branches. On down the hills of slime and through the rivers of mud.

Occasionally he had to rest and tune in to Ballantyre Road. Exhausted, all of them except

Henry had fallen asleep at the kitchen table. Henry sang. In a croaky voice he sang every song he knew and several he made up. He sang 'Bananas in Pyjamas'. He sang 'Nellie the Elephant'. He sang 'Do Your Ears Hang Low?' Harvey Angell closed his eyes and listened. And Henry's young voice, with the ache of hope in it, gave him just enough Energy to struggle on.

★ ★ ★

Just before dawn, when they were all awake again and Mr Perkins, in desperation was preparing to read either the dictionary or the telephone directory, they heard slow, tired footsteps coming up the path.

Henry rushed to open the door. Harvey Angell, with Sweetheart asleep against his chest, staggered in. But a changed Harvey Angell. His sky-blue suit was as grey as his exhausted face. His eyes had lost all joy. He couldn't manage the smallest smile.

Outside the door, the hollyhocks drooped as if in urgent need of water.

CHAPTER 15

It was Mrs Sowerby who took them all in hand
that Sunday morning. She observed the curtains
of 131 drawn all morning and the house curiously still and silent. None of the usual comings
and goings. No Sweetheart out in her pram.

Driven – this time by a kindly curiosity – Mrs
Sowerby knocked on the front door and got no
reply. She noticed the drooping hollyhocks and
made a mental note to water them later. She
went round to the back door. Still no reply. But
there was a kitchen window open.

Mrs Sowerby was neither small nor agile. She
was also a law-abiding citizen. Climbing through
someone else's window could well be classified
as breaking and entering. She pushed the
window up a little and peered inside. She saw
the Connecting Kit and a muddle of mugs, half-
eaten sandwiches and books on the kitchen
table, and no sign of anybody.

Needs must, thought Mrs Sowerby and, hit-
ching up her skirts and trying a few experimental

jumps, she heaved herself onto the windowsill and then half-rolled, half-fell inside.

Once in, she was unsure what to do next. But the matter was solved for her by Miss Muggins appearing. Miss Muggins with bags under her eyes and still in the clothes she'd fallen asleep in. Miss Muggins gave a squeak of alarm when she saw Mrs Sowerby, and Mrs Sowerby, blushing, was quick to explain.

"I was worried about you all," she said. "The curtains drawn and the house so quiet. I climbed in." She gestured to the open kitchen window.

After all that had been happening, and after the night's adventures, a neighbour climbing in the window seemed a perfectly normal happening to Miss Muggins.

"Cup of tea?" she asked, moving towards the kettle.

"Well, yes," said Mrs Sowerby, "but let me make it. You look done in."

"Done in. Yes," said Miss Muggins. "We all are. What a night!"

Mrs Sowerby, who in the last couple of weeks had had time to reflect on the nature of her curiosity, had resolved not to ask too many questions. But now she couldn't resist.

"What happened?" she asked.

"Kidnapped," said Miss Muggins, too tired to make long sentences. "Sweetheart. By Ghost Mothers. Rescued. By Harvey Angell. Both very poorly. Night night," and Miss Muggins' head sank onto the table.

"Good heavens!" said Mrs Sowerby, stirring an extra spoon of sugar into the tea and setting it before Miss Muggins who woke enough to take a few sips.

Something else had happened to Mrs Sowerby since she'd met Harvey Angell. Her imagination had woken up and so had that hunger for love which, over the years, had been twisted into nosiness and Thinking-Unpleasant-Thoughts-About-Other-People. Now Mrs Sowerby didn't bat an eye at the mention of kidnapping and Ghost Mothers. Instead she thought, 'I am needed here.'

"You go back to bed," she told Miss Muggins. "I'm going to bring everyone breakfast in bed."

"Very kind. Very kind," said Miss Muggins, drifting towards the stairs, almost asleep on her feet. "Sweetheart. Carrot juice. In fridge."

"Don't worry about a thing," Mrs Sowerby called after her and then set to. She cleared the kitchen table. She found trays, bowls, spoons. She made porridge and toast. More tea. She had to hurry back to the kitchen for a sixth tray when she discovered Rosie, who'd stayed the night, asleep on the floor in Henry's room.

They were all very grateful. Aunt Agatha said she couldn't remember when she'd last had breakfast in bed. Mr Perkins, astonished and shy, spilt his tea and mopped it up with a corner of his sheet when Mrs Sowerby left his room. Henry and Rosie hardly said anything other than

"Wow!" and "Wicked!" before tucking into their large bowls of porridge.

"Don't wake Mr Angell and Sweetheart," said Aunt Agatha. "They both need more sleep."

But Mrs Sowerby didn't think she could have woken them even if she'd wanted to, they were both so deeply asleep. Henry and Rosie between them ate Harvey Angell's breakfast.

Mrs Sowerby collected up the empty bowls and plates, washed everything up and felt deeply satisfied. Reluctant to leave, she mopped the kitchen floor and watered the hollyhocks. They seemed to perk up a little.

By mid-afternoon the others were all up and dressed – all that is except Harvey Angell and Sweetheart. They slept on. Mrs Sowerby went home and decided to do some baking. All of them over there at 131 looked as if they could do with some home cooking, she thought. And although she didn't wish to think an Unpleasant Thought, Mrs Sowerby felt that home cooking wasn't one of Aunt Agatha's talents.

By tea-time Harvey Angell was awake but too weak, it seemed, to get out of bed. They all fussed about him. Miss Muggins brought him her very own knitted bed jacket because he was so shivery. Rosie gave him her old and much-loved panda who was rather worn about the ears but nevertheless had a very kindly expression. Mr Perkins brought him *The Poetical Works of William Blake*, saying (rather shyly) that there was no need for Harvey Angell to actually *read* it, he was sure that just patting the cover would be beneficial. Harvey Angell gave a wan smile and said he was sure Mr Perkins was right. Miss Skivvy filled and re-filled hot water bottles. Aunt Agatha tried to tempt Harvey Angell's appetite with soup, boiled eggs, jelly and ice cream, but everything went back to the kitchen untouched. Henry became the Expert Plumper of Pillows.

They were all even more worried about Sweetheart. Sweetheart slept on. This, by itself, was not a cause for concern. They all agreed that sleep was a great healer and that after her experience with the Ghost Mothers, sleep was what Sweetheart needed.

It was her colour – or lack of it – that worried them. There was something rather grey – 'ashen' Miss Skivvy called it – about her complexion, and a slightly shrivelled look about her face. They'd brought Sweetheart's cot into the kitchen so that someone could be with her all the time. Henry tried to tell himself that he was imagining wrinkles where dimples had been. He wasn't cheered when Rosie said, "She looks sort of – old. She's got a little old lady's face."

"She's just recovering," Henry snapped. "You'd look like that after a night with the Ghost Mothers." And Rosie fell silent, reminded, again, that it was all her fault. "Who knows what Sweetheart's been through," said Henry.

None of them felt able to ask Harvey Angell this for he was obviously too poorly.

"Talking about it might make him feel worse,"

said Aunt Agatha. "Perhaps when he's better he'll tell us."

But during the night, Harvey Angell became feverish. His temperature soared almost beyond the reach of the mercury in the thermometer. Miss Muggins wrapped bags of frozen peas in tea towels and cooled his forehead, but still Harvey Angell tossed and turned. Sometimes he dozed and began talking about mud, mud, mud. Once he sang a little of 'Rock-a-bye-baby' and groaned terribly.

"Delirious," said Aunt Agatha. "I'm going to call the doctor."

But at that Harvey Angell struggled to sit up and speak.

"What is it?" asked Henry. "How can we help?"

"No doctor," whispered Harvey Angell. "Fetch Gabriel."

CHAPTER 16

It was the middle of the night. The second sleepless one. In the kitchen of 131 Ballantyre Road all eyes turned to Henry and Mr Perkins.

It should be known that although Aunt Agatha could thrive very well on five hours' sleep a night, Mr Perkins was a grumbling wreck on less than eight and preferably ten.

"The Waifs and Strays Café," said Henry. "That's the only way we know to reach Gabriel."

"*If* it's open at three in the morning," said Mr Perkins, "and *if* Gabriel is there, and *if* we've got the right sort of Energy to find the café, which I doubt." Tiredness made Mr Perkins tetchy. "Surely," he wheedled, while a picture of his soft, plump, snuggable duvet rose in his mind, "Dr Quirk would do just as well? I mean a fever's a fever, isn't it?"

"Perkins," said Aunt Agatha reaching for her hat and coat and handing Henry his anorak, "I'm ashamed of you. If Harvey Angell says he needs Gabriel, then it's Gabriel he needs and Gabriel he shall have." (For once Henry wanted to cheer his tough and gallant aunt.) "Henry," she continued, "go and see if Mr Angell can possibly give us just a word of advice about how to find this café."

Henry tiptoed back into the sitting room where Harvey Angell lay. "Mr Angell," he whispered. "We're going to fetch Gabriel, but please can you tell us how to find the café?"

Harvey Angell opened his eyes. Henry thought he had never seen anyone look so tired. "In my bag, Henry. In the pocket. A card," said Harvey Angell and closed his eyes again.

Henry found the bag in which Harvey Angell kept his Connecting Kit and his silver flute. There was indeed a small pocket at the front, and inside it a card.

The card said: 'FAIR CHANCE CAB COMPANY. TRANSPORT YOU ANY-WHERE.' It was followed by a long telephone number. Henry ran back into the kitchen and handed the card to Aunt Agatha.

"Fair Chance," said Aunt Agatha, dialing the telephone number. "I'm not sure I like the sound of that."

The telephone was answered at once by a voice saying, "Fair Chance Cab Company. Chancey speaking. How can I help you?"

"Oh, er, well," began Aunt Agatha, suddenly feeling rather foolish, "my nephew and I want to go to The Waifs and Strays Café."

"No problem, darling," said Mr Chancey. "Be

with you in two ticks of a meter." And the line went dead.

"But I haven't told him where we are!" wailed Aunt Agatha.

"No need, I think," said Mr Perkins, who had begun to feel he was missing out, "I can hear a car coming now."

And when they looked out of the window, there it was, a bright yellow cab with 'Fair Chance Cab Co.' written on the side and a neon sign on the roof that said 'Adventures Only'. Briefly the headlights lit up the hollyhocks, upright now and straight as soldiers on sentry duty.

Mr Chancey tooted his horn (bringing Mrs Sowerby to her window) and, keeping the engine going, stepped out of the driver's seat and opened the passenger's door with a flourish. Mr Chancey was an extremely elegant man. He wore a purple and pink waistcoat, a floating silk scarf and tiny round specs.

Aunt Agatha delivered her last orders. "Perkins, look after Mr Angell. Muggins, Skivvy, stay with Sweetheart." Then they were off.

Mr Chancey's name matched his driving. He drove very fast with one careless hand on the wheel. His silk scarf flew from the open window like a flag fluttering from a turret. He sang as he drove, ignoring several sets of traffic lights and his brake pedal.

"Might I inquire," asked Aunt Agatha holding on to her hat which also threatened to blow out of the window, "why you call your company The Fair Chance Cab Company?"

"Chancey by name, chancey by nature, darling. There's a fair chance we'll get there and a fair chance we won't. All life's a chance, don't you think, darling?"

Aunt Agatha wasn't really up to thinking anything. She'd begun to feel slightly sick. Henry was very glad that the streets were empty. Close to the centre of town Mr Chancey switched on his siren. It sounded very much like that of an ambulance.

"Do we really need that?" shouted Aunt Agatha.

"This is an emergency, isn't it, darling?" shouted Mr Chancey.

"I suppose it is," shouted Aunt Agatha. "But there isn't any traffic."

"Give us a break, darling. I don't often get to use this." And taking a few corners at a speed that threw Aunt Agatha and Henry into a heap, Mr Chancey carried on singing, 'You Are My Sunshine, My Only Sunshine'.

Aunt Agatha put her fingers in her ears and closed her eyes. But the fast ride, the silent starlit streets made Henry feel exhilarated, full of young, spring-like energy.

With a much-practised dramatic screech of brakes, Mr Chancey pulled up outside The Waifs and Strays Café. And yes! The lights were still on and yes, there were people inside.

With a final wave and a toot, Mr Chancey

drove off. Aunt Agatha adjusted her hat and patted her chest like one about to make a speech at a village fête. Resolutely she approached the door of the Waifs and Strays Café. But although the lights were on and they could see people in the booths, the door wouldn't open.

"The waitress," said Henry. "She'll recognise me and let us in." And he banged on the door.

But the waitress who opened it was a different one. She was large and dark-haired. "There's a private function going on here," she said, opening the door a mere crack. "Meeting of Homer Elders. That's obviously not you, is it?" And she was about to close the door on them, only Aunt Agatha had put her foot firmly in the crack.

Aunt Agatha assumed her most hoity-toity manner. "If you don't mind, young lady," she said, "we've come to see Mr Gabriel on a matter of urgent business." And without waiting for a reply, Aunt Agatha pushed the door open and marched Henry in before her.

They didn't need to find Gabriel. He spotted Henry at once and with a look of alarm immediately came towards them, reaching out to clasp Henry's hands.

"Henry! Is everything all right? Harvey Angell . . . he hasn't . . .?" but Gabriel left the sentence unfinished.

Aunt Agatha took over. "I'm Henry's aunt," she said, "and everything is not at all all right.

116

Far from it. Mr Angell is very poorly and asking for you."

"And Sweetheart's poorly too," added Henry. "At least she's not quite herself."

"I'll come at once," said Gabriel. "Just let me fetch my bag."

Gabriel had his own form of transport. It was a motor bike with a side-car. After some uncertainty on Aunt Agatha's part, she climbed in the side car and Henry (with a slightly over-large helmet on his head) went on the back.

Clinging on to Gabriel, and over the noise of the engine, he tried to explain what had happened. How Sweetheart had been snatched by the Ghost Mothers. How Harvey Angell had gone to the City of Shadows to rescue her. How he had come back grey and weak with exhaustion and that now he had developed a fever.

If Mr Chancey had driven fast, Gabriel drove even faster. The side-car fairly bounced along. "Balloons, taxis, motor bikes," moaned Aunt Agatha. "Never again."

It was dawn when they got back to Ballantyre Road. The milkman looked at them in surprise. "Out on the town?" he asked Aunt Agatha.

"In a manner of speaking," Aunt Agatha snapped and whisked three bottles of milk out of his arms.

They took Gabriel straight to Harvey Angell's room. Mr Perkins had fallen asleep in an armchair but he jumped up, all groggy and confused, when they came in.

"Is it morning already?" he asked. "He's been talking in his sleep again. Something about a Lake of Tears. And there was a bit of a nonsense song. 'Halibu, crackabu', something like that. I couldn't make head nor tail of it."

"Still very feverish," said Gabriel laying a hand on Harvey Angell's forehead. "How are you, my good fellow?" he asked as Harvey Angell opened his eyes.

"Spin, span, muskidan, twiddle-um, twaddle-um, twenty one," Harvey Angell replied.

"Umm," said Gabriel. "I need to test his Energy Level." He produced from his bag what looked very like the armband and pump doctor's use to test blood pressure. Only Gabriel had two small bands and these he wound round Harvey Angell's feet.

"Always the feet," said Gabriel. "Energy comes from the earth, rises to the feet. It's as I thought. He's low. Very low."

"What can we do?" asked Henry anxiously. "Is there a medicine he can take to make him better?"

"Or something like a blood transfusion," suggested Mr Perkins.

Gabriel smiled. "That's nearer the mark," he said. "All is not lost. I'm going to write a prescription."

It was the strangest prescription any of them had ever seen and certainly not available from a chemist.

Gabriel's prescription read like this:

Music – to be taken three times a day.

Cheerful chat – regularly every four hours.

Company of children – frequent. ("That's you and Rosie," Mr Perkins said to Henry.)

A poem a day. (Mr Perkins beamed a beam of almost as many kilowatts as Harvey Angell's own.)

Dietary Requirements: soup, fruit crumble, shortbread, pancakes, fresh fruit, occasional chocolate biscuit/cake. Irn Bru.

"Good heavens!" said Aunt Agatha, looking at the list. "It'll be non-stop cooking. And cost a fortune," she muttered.

"And," said Gabriel, reaching into his bag for a bottle of purple liquid "give him a teaspoon of this every morning. That should re-charge him. Have him zapping with Energy in a matter of days. Now then, let me look at the child."

Sweetheart was awake now. She lay still in her cot. She didn't smile as she usually did when Henry reached down to tickle her tummy.

"She hasn't bleeped or smiled all night," said Miss Skivvy.

"And she won't drink anything," said Miss Muggins.

"She still looks grey," said Aunt Agatha.

Very tenderly Gabriel lifted Sweetheart from her cot. Sweetheart screwed up her face as if she was trying to smile but couldn't quite manage it. She rested her head against Gabriel's broad chest and gave the faintest sigh.

"I'm afraid this is bad," said Gabriel. "Sweetheart has a very serious disease."

"What is it?" cried Henry. "What's the matter with her? Shall I call an ambulance?"

Gabriel put his hand on Henry's shoulder. "There isn't really a cure for Sweetheart's kind of illness," he said.

"Nonsense," dared Aunt Agatha. "Medical science can do wonders these day."

"Not for this, I fear," said Gabriel. "You see Sweetheart's disease is loneliness."

"She *can't* be lonely!" Henry protested, taking Sweetheart from Gabriel's arms and hugging her. "She can't be lonely. She's got us. All of us." ('And particularly me,' he was thinking.)

"It's hard to understand," said Gabriel, "but she's lonely for her kith and kin. For her own people and her own time."

"Her mother," said Miss Muggins beginning to cry.

"Yes, indeed," said Gabriel. "The thing is, every child is born with an immediate supply of mother love. Sweetheart has thrived on that. But it's as I expected. She's beginning to run out."

Miss Muggins broke down completely. "That's the saddest thing I've ever heard," she wailed.

"There must be something we can do," said Henry desperately.

"We really need Sweetheart's mother to come for her," said Gabriel. And soon. Very soon. Or else . . ." but one look at their faces stopped him saying more.

Wildly Henry tugged at Gabriel's arm. "But if she doesn't come, if she can't find the crack in time then . . ." Henry's voice broke, "then Harvey Angell can take her. Back to her mother. He said he could do it! He said he could!"

Gabriel looked sadly at Harvey Angell, pale and feverish in his bed. "Yes," he said with a great sigh. "When he's well again, he *could* do it."

"I think I can hear a 'but'," said Aunt Agatha.

Gabriel smiled sadly. "But," he continued, "he'd have to feel the magnetic pull of Sweetheart's mother. That means we'd need to know which country Sweetheart has come from. Even with that knowledge, it would still be a very dangerous mission."

"He could do it!" said Henry stoutly. "I know he could do it!"

"The dangers of the past are known," said Gabriel, putting a gentle hand on Henry's shoulder. "Those of the future, unknown."

CHAPTER 17

They were all so tired, so anxious about Harvey Angell and Sweetheart, so bothered by the thought of unknown dangers of the future, that they quite forgot about the dangers of the present. About PC 45 and PC 16. About the fear that Sweetheart would be taken away and put 'in care'.

Then one morning there was a knock on the door and a young woman who introduced herself as Miss Stella Maris of the Child Protection Unit, stood on the doorstep.

It was Stella's first day in the job and her first ever visit. She was just twenty-one, fair-haired and dreamy. 'Dozey', according to her father who was always saying that it was time Stella woke up to 'the real world'. Stella's friends said much the same. 'Stella, get real,' they said. But Stella's dreaminess was such that she had no idea what was involved in 'getting real', how to do it or how to know when you *had* done it.

Becoming a social worker had seemed a good start, but Stella hadn't found it easy. She had failed her exams three times and only just passed on the fourth attempt. For several weeks she had accompanied other social workers on visits to families. Now here she was in Ballantyre Road, on her own and with what seemed like a very odd report from her superior on a child called Sweetheart Angell.

It read as follows:–

SWEETHEART ANGELL: approx. 3 months old.

Query: stolen.

Neighbour reports strange physical features.

Query: feelers. *Query*: bleeping.

Uncertain parentage.

Father thought to be one H. Angell of no fixed abode.

Query: family dysfunctional. (Claim baby found under hollyhocks.)

Query: psychiatric report.

Stella had read this report over and over without it making any sense. On the doorstep of 131 she eyed the hollyhocks which nodded at her as if to say 'we know what you're about'. Stella nodded back.

It was Mrs Sowerby who opened the door. Mrs Sowerby in a vast flowery apron, a wooden spoon in one hand and, drifting out from behind her, a delicious smell of scones, apple crumble, possibly chocolate cake.

If anyone had measured Mrs Sowerby's

Energy Level that Friday afternoon they would probably have found that it had gone right off the scale. With so many people to look after, Mrs Sowerby had never felt so happy.

"I'm from Social Services . . ." Stella began.

"Come in!" cried Mrs Sowerby. She had entirely forgotten her report to the police. That episode seemed to belong to a past Mrs Sowerby, a Mrs Sowerby she had tossed off like a worn-out dress.

"From the Child Protection Unit," Stella continued.

"Ah, then you've come to see Sweetheart," said Mrs Sowerby cheerfully. "The dearest little thing, but rather poorly at the moment. I expect that's why you're here. I'm looking after everyone you know."

"And you are . . .?" Stella had her notebook ready. ('Make sure you take notes,' she'd been told.)

"Mrs Sowerby, dear. Friend and neighbour. Stepping in in an hour of need."

"Need?" queried Stella. Could this be the neighbour who had made the report to the police? Surely not.

"Mr Angell and Sweetheart, both being poorly. I thought you'd have known that, dear. And everyone else exhausted. Just exhausted. Such a lovely family too. Excuse me. My scones! You'd better come into the kitchen."

"So, not a dysfunctional family?" Stella ventured.

"Dys-what?" said Mrs Sowerby, hands on her hips. "Let me tell you this, my girl. We may not be your average family here, but you'd be hard pressed to find a home with – with more love floating around in it." And Mrs Sowerby waved her hands in the air as if love could be seen, floating like dust particles in the air above them. Stella looked up and fancied she saw them.

She considered the report again. "It says here that the baby was found under the hollyhocks," she said hesitantly.

"So what!" said Mrs Sowerby, whose loyalty to everyone at 131 was now unswerving and unquestioning. "Moses was found in a basket, wasn't he?"

"I suppose he was," said Stella, wondering if this was how the Real World operated. "Perhaps I could meet the family," she suggested, "and have a look at Sweetheart" ('Do *not* leave the house without seeing the child,' she'd been instructed.)

"All having an afternoon nap," said Mrs Sowerby. "I packed them off. 'No arguing', I said. 'You all need your sleep.' "

"I see," said Stella, who didn't. "But I've got to write a report. If I could just see Sweetheart and perhaps the child's father?"

"Father?"

"Mr Angell. I understand he's the father. It says 'of no fixed abode' here, but I take it he's come home?"

"Home? Everywhere's home to Harvey

125

Angell," said Mrs Sowerby. "He's quite the nicest gentleman you could ever meet," she added.

"I'm sure," said Stella. Who wasn't at all sure. Of anything.

"Well, I suppose there's no harm in letting you have a quick look at them," said Mrs Sowerby. "We've put them together, the two poorly ones. But not too many questions, mind. Mr Angell has to have plenty of rest, music and fruit crumble."

"Of course," said Stella. "I'll try to be quick and quiet."

Going into the living room, with Mrs Sowerby shushing Stella at every step, they looked first at Sweetheart. Although still not her rosy self, Sweetheart was obviously well cared for. She was wearing her prettiest nightie (handmade and embroidered by Miss Muggins). Two teddies (presents from Mr Perkins and Rosie) sat at the bottom of her cot. On a chair beside her were stacks of nappies, neatly folded, clean cardigans and dresses, her bonnets and a shawl. Sweetheart wasn't well enough either to bleep or to pop her feelers out but she opened her eyes and gave a tiny smile.

"She's lovely," said Stella. "And I can see she's very well cared for."

"The little duck," said Mrs Sowerby fondly.

Their voices woke Harvey Angell. "I'll introduce you," whispered Mrs Sowerby, "but not too many questions, mind."

But there was no need for introductions. Seeing Stella, Harvey Angell pulled himself up in bed and at once took her hand.

Stella felt a small electric shock run up her arm and down again.

"I knew it!" said Harvey Angell. "As soon as you walked in, I knew it. Mrs Sowerby, my dear, would you be so kind . . ."

Mrs Sowerby, who had been gawping at the pair of them, blinked fast and stood up straight. "Oh yes. I'll leave you to it. If that's all right with you, Mr Angell?"

"The moment you came into the room I could feel it," said Harvey Angell, still holding Stella's hand. "The Energy, a kind of sea energy in your case, coursing through. Hasn't anyone told you?"

"Told me?" Leaning close to Harvey Angell, Stella had the curious feeling that she had known him all her life, that in a way she couldn't name, they were connected.

"Why," said Harvey Angell, "that you're one of us. A budding Homer. Of course very budding. Very junior. But still. Now listen. This is what you must do. Report to Gabriel at the Waifs and Strays Café. Tell him I sent you. Have you got that?"

And Stella heard herself laughing. Laughing as if everything was now explained. As if at last she was out in the Real World. Her own real world.

Mrs Sowerby watched her skip down the path,

nod at the hollyhocks, toss her notebook into a convenient wheelie bin and vanish.

"No accounting for folk," said Mrs Sowerby, shaking her head and deciding it was time to wake everyone up with tea and scones.

* * *

Fed and fussed over by Mrs Sowerby, they were soon able to give Harvey Angell and Sweetheart what Mr Perkins called "Full-On TLC". ('Tender Loving Care,' Henry explained to Miss Muggins.)

Gabriel's prescription for Harvey Angell was followed to the letter. Every morning he was given a teaspoon of the purplish medicine.

"It looks like concentrate of hollyhock," said Aunt Agatha.

"That's not what it says on the label," said Miss Skivvy. "It says 'sapientia serpens et lucis vitae' – whatever that is."

"Latin," said Mr Perkins. "Meaning 'snake wisdom and light of life'."

"Wicked!" said Rosie.

They pushed the piano into the sitting room so that Harvey Angell could have his regular dose of music three times a day. Sometimes Aunt Agatha played by herself. Sometimes they all gathered round to sing and Harvey Angell, though not well enough to join in with his flute, beat time with an imaginary baton.

'Cheerful chat' wasn't quite so easy. Often

they were too worried about Sweetheart's wan little face to be truly cheerful and then Mrs Sowerby had to take over, though Aunt Agatha expressed doubts about Mrs Sowerby's street gossip being always what you could call 'cheerful chat'.

"I don't think the story of Mr Brown's bunions could be called 'cheerful'," said Aunt Agatha.

"Ah, but I tell it in a cheerful way," said Mrs Sowerby.

Mr Perkins had a wonderful time choosing and reciting a poem a day.

"Make sure they're *comforting* poems," said Aunt Agatha. "No laments or dirges." So Mr Perkins had to swop 'Ode to Melancholy' (one of his favourites) for 'Infant Joy' and 'Lament for the Makers' for 'Jabberwocky', which made Harvey Angell laugh.

Nor could Mr Perkins resist adding a poem of his own. It was a Get-Well-Soon sort of poem and had, as its refrain:

No summer can outshine your smile –
Get well! We need your spark and style.

Henry and Rosie between them easily supplied that part of the prescription that required 'the company of children'. They sat on the bottom of his bed and played Ludo and Scrabble and Snakes and Ladders and throughout every game Henry worried about the unknown dangers of the future.

"You are not to ask him," said Aunt Agatha. "Not until he's fit and well."

Day by day they watched him recover. They didn't need to take his temperature. They could tell it by the hollyhocks which budded and bloomed as if it was high summer and a heat-wave. They lifted their broad flappy wings like the skirts of girls about to dance. Henry half expected them to uproot and fly for they looked so very healthy. And by the following week so did Harvey Angell.

If only they had been able to apply Gabriel's prescription to Sweetheart as well as Harvey Angell, thought Henry. But they couldn't. They rocked her, sang to her, tickled her toes, kissed her more times than anyone could count, took her for walks in the park, jigged her on their knees, playing 'round and round the garden' on her hands and 'this little piggy' on her toes, tried to tempt her with all manner of vegetable juices from mango to tomato . . . but nothing worked.

Sweetheart began to lose weight. Her face was not exactly sad, but she looked as if she was listening in to something far, far away.

"Perhaps she can hear her mother calling," said Rosie.

"Perhaps," said Harvey Angell. "But time's running out. We daren't wait much longer."

CHAPTER 18

No-one could comfort Henry, though everyone tried. School had begun again after the Easter holidays and teacher after teacher was driven to say, "Henry, will you *please* pay attention."

But Henry's attention was elsewhere. It was on Sweetheart and Sweetheart's missing mother. He kept trying to picture the Crack in Time through which Sweetheart had slipped. A shaft of sunlight, Harvey Angell had said, and a knife-like blade of light and down, down, down through time she'd come. And now Sweetheart's mother, out there in the twenty-third century, was trying to find just such another crack. She might, at this very moment, have already slipped through and be wandering the world, looking for Sweetheart.

This notion took such a hold on Henry that he found himself staring at any woman who happened to be standing in a patch of sunlight. Could this be she, Sweetheart's mother?

"Want to take a photograph, love?" asked one young woman standing outside the newsagent's in a halo of sunshine. Henry blushed and hurried home.

Harvey Angell was often out. "Gone to the café," Aunt Agatha said. "To see if there's any reports on the Fabulor of mothers looking for babies."

Once or twice Henry had found Harvey Angell studying a chunky manual with the strange title, *Navigational Problems and Energy Consumption*. Most evenings now they set up the Connecting Kit and Century Clock on the kitchen table and picked up the Energy Track to the twenty-third century.

"Gabriel says that if there's interference, we might be able to tell which country it's coming from," said Harvey Angell. But although the Clock confirmed that the twenty-third century was Sweetheart's time, there was nothing to tell them of her place.

"Global," said Mr Perkins. "Everything might be so global in a couple of centuries that there won't be countries any more. Just continents."

"Even a continent would narrow things down a bit," said Harvey Angell and went back to his manual.

Meanwhile Sweetheart grew paler and thinner. They noticed that she was often cold, even though it was now early May and warm. She already had plenty of woolly cardigans, but Miss Muggins knitted more. Miss Muggins knitted fast and furiously. She knitted as if she was knitting magic spells into the wool. Spells to make Sweetheart better.

At night Sweetheart now slept mainly in Henry's room, only she didn't sleep much any more. Nor did Henry. He would wake suddenly in the night, switch on his bedside light and see Sweetheart with her eyes open, looking at him. Sometimes she would reach up her arms, meaning that she wanted a cuddle. And sometimes Henry had the curious feeling that she was looking after him as much as he was looking after her and the thought came to him that before Sweetheart, the door to his heart had been – well, maybe half shut. And now it was wide open.

Henry's sadness was mixed with fear. He knew that Harvey Angell was making preparations. Firstly there was the manual with the difficult title. And then he'd seen Harvey Angell checking the hot air balloon which, since his arrival in Ballantyre Road, had been packed in a bag like a huge pillow case, and left in the garden. Lastly there were the 'unknown dangers' that both Gabriel and Harvey Angell refused to talk about.

Henry had it fixed in his mind that Harvey Angell could do anything. But could he beat time itself? What *were* the dangers and what if he were to lose both Sweetheart *and* Harvey Angell? It was too awful to think about and much too awful to talk about.

Mr Perkins, guessing how Henry felt, tried to

comfort him. "Sweetheart has been a joy to us all," said Mr Perkins. "D'you know what Blake says about joy, Henry?"

"No," said Henry glumly and not much wanting to know.

> "He who bends to himself a Joy
> Doth the wingèd life destroy;
> But he who kisses the Joy as it flies
> Lives in Eternity's sunrise."

But Henry cared nothing for Eternity. The twenty-third century was quite distant enough.

Rosie didn't do much better in trying to cheer him. She brought round her stamp collection and gave him half. But Henry only looked moodily at stamps from Italy, Africa, America, and wondered if one of these countries was Sweetheart's home.

It was Rosie who found out.

★　★　★

Left to her own devices, Rosie took to going to the park alone after school. She sat on the swing she had swung on with Sweetheart when the Ghost Mother had appeared, and thought about things.

Rosie thought that she and Henry would be friends for ever and that if it hadn't been for Sweetheart their friendship might never have happened.

So thought Rosie, swinging gently, knowing

that she too would miss Sweetheart badly while thinking of names for the ten babies of her own she was planning.

Then she saw her. The very same Ghost Mother who had snatched Sweetheart away. She was lurking in the shadows of a vast Lebanon Cedar, its sweeping branches making a kind of cave.

Rosie froze. Why was she here? Was she hoping to steal Sweetheart again? Rosie was just about to make a dash for it when the Ghost Mother beckoned her.

Walk away, Rosie told herself. Just walk quietly away. Don't run. Don't look. But she couldn't help herself. The Ghost Mother beckoned again, this time more urgently and Rosie, telling herself that perhaps the Ghost Mother had a message from Sweetheart's real mother, found herself walking towards her, ducking her head under the curtains made by the tree's branches, until they were both standing inside a cave of green shadow.

The Ghost Mother tried to take Rosie's hand. Rosie pulled away.

"I just came to tell you," whispered the Ghost Mother with tears in her eyes.

"What?" demanded Rosie, though her legs were shaking.

"That I'm sorry, sorry, sorry," said the Ghost Mother.

"I should think so too," said Rosie, the way her mother said it when she, Rosie, said sorry for leaving her room a mess or forgetting to take her packed lunch to school.

The Ghost Mother looked about her as if afraid of being overheard. Then before Rosie could pull back, she grabbed her hand. "Tell him!" she said. "Tell him, Merimbula!"

"Merimbula?" echoed Rosie, but the Ghost Mother had gone.

CHAPTER 19

For a moment Rosie remained standing under the shadow of the cedar tree as if her feet were rooted like the tree's trunk. Then in a dazed kind of way she began walking through the park saying, "Merimbula, Merimbula," over and over as if the word was as puzzling, or magical, as abracadabra.

It was a sunny afternoon and it seemed as if everyone had come out to enjoy it. A group of students lazed on the grass drinking Coke and laughing. A few boys had set up a game of football. Dogs were out for an afternoon romp, toddlers toddled, old age pensioners sat on the benches warming their bones. A skateboarder came whizzing gracefully down one of the paths, and the cherry and horse chestnut trees, as if to join in what felt like the beginning of spring, put out buds and white candles.

"Merimbula, Merimbula, Merimbula," said Rosie out loud so that several people looked at her as if she was very strange. Rosie reached the park gates and suddenly understood.

"MERIMBULA!" she shouted. "That's it!" And she ran. Ran until she was breathless and banging on the door of 131 Ballantrye Road, hopping up and down with impatience on the doorstep. The hollyhocks hopped too as if to say 'we knew this all along.'

"Merimbula!" said Rosie to an astonished looking Henry, and rushed past him into the kitchen. Harvey Angell was playing his flute to Sweetheart. Harvey Angell's flute seemed to be the only thing that soothed Sweetheart. She lay on a rug and wriggled her toes to the tune.

"Merimbula!" Rosie shouted again. "She told me. The Ghost Mother. I met her again. She told me to tell you."

At once Harvey Angell put down his flute. "An atlas," he cried. "Who's got an atlas?"

Miss Skivvy produced one. "I go bedtime-travelling with this," she said. But no-one wanted to hear about Miss Skivvy's bedtime travels just then. Harvey Angell began running his finger down the Ms in the index.

Miss Skivvy looked doubtfully over his shoulder. "Why would a Ghost Mother know where Sweetheart came from?" she asked.

"That's easy," said Harvey Angell. "The Ghost Mothers have a network. They can sometimes find out things we can never learn. They rarely tell. We're lucky."

His finger continued down the index. "Merida, Spain," he read. "Meriden, Wyoming. Meridian, Mississipi. Merigny, France.

Merikavia, Finland. MERIMBULA – New South Wales, Australia!"

And at this Sweetheart kicked her feet in the air and gave a tiny bleep – the first for many days. Harvey Angell gave Rosie a huge hug. "You're a genius!" he said. Rosie blushed and smiled. "It was nothing," she said.

"Tomorrow morning, first light," said Harvey Angell. "Balloon launch. I want everyone ready."

In his bedroom that night, Henry looked sadly at Sweetheart. She slept contentedly, as if she knew she was going home. Home to her own time and her own place.

"I know how it is to want your mother," Henry whispered. Then he cried himself to sleep.

* * *

When Henry woke up, Harvey Angell was already out in the back garden with Mr Perkins, checking the balloon.

Apart from Harvey Angell, no-one, it seemed, felt like any breakfast, despite the appearance of Mrs Sowerby with warm croissants and home-made marmalade. Harvey Angell ate several.

Henry sat beside him, trying to put into words the question it hurt to ask. "How dangerous is it?" he asked. "You taking Sweetheart into the future?"

Harvey Angell waved a buttery knife in the air. "Well, I've been on safer missions," he said.

"But let me tell you a secret, Henry. Between you and me, I like a little danger. It's the tang in the marmalade, the nip in the air on a frosty morning, it's the buzz you get when you know there's a risk."

"But how *big* a risk," persisted Henry.

Harvey Angell finished a final croissant and walked Henry outside. They sat on the front doorstep close to the hollyhocks. The balloon was packed up and waiting. Harvey Angell put an arm round Henry's shoulder. "The thing is," he said, "the routes to the past are all well-travelled. You could say the past is well lived-in. Homely, if you like. But the future . . . the path's unknown, uncertain."

"Can you be sure of getting there?" pressed Henry.

There was a long silence. "No," said Harvey Angell at last. "I wish I could tell you I *was* sure, Henry. But there's a point when you just have to believe and hope."

"Hope?"

"Hope that you've got enough love – enough Energy to get you through. You all love Sweetheart enough to want her happiness. That'll help. I can draw Energy from that."

Henry pondered. "But you will come back, won't you?" he asked.

"It rather depends on my having enough Energy to get there *and* back," said Harvey Angell. "But I don't think I want to hang about in the twenty-third century, I've got to keep an eye on you, you know."

There was no time for more questions. To Henry's surprise a yellow taxi drew up with a trailer attached to the back, and there was Mr Chancey in his pink and purple waistcoat and floaty silk scarf. And besides Mr Chancey was Stella Maris, looking as bright as morning itself and wearing a cap that seemed made of silver tinsel.

Harvey Angell hurried to greet them. Henry, watching the trio, was suddenly reminded of the 'customers' in the Waifs and Strays Café. All of them looked as if that was where they belonged.

Mrs Sowerby squinted at Stella Maris. "I've seen that girl before somewhere," she muttered, "only I can't quite remember..."

"Let me introduce you to Stella Maris," Harvey Angell interrupted, "a rising star in the Homer world and someone who is going to be very useful to us."

"But wasn't she... didn't she...?" began Mrs Sowerby.

But Mr Chancey interrupted this time, leaping out of his cab and calling, "Morning, darling!" to Aunt Agatha and to Harvey Angell, "Grand flying weather. Want a hand with that balloon?"

"Please could someone tell me where we're going?" asked Miss Muggins. "And I trust I don't have to go up in that thing."

"We're going to the country," said Harvey

141

Angell. "I shall be flying with Sweetheart but I'll need your help for the launch."

After they'd loaded the balloon into the trailer, they all climbed into Mr Chancey's taxi. Although it was large, it was still a squeeze getting everyone in. In the back, Henry, with Sweetheart on his knee, sat squashed between Aunt Agatha and Mr Perkins. Rosie (who insisted on coming) had to sit on Mr Perkins' knee. Facing them, on the fold-up seats, were Miss Skivvy and Miss Muggins.

Harvey Angell sat in the front between Mr Chancey and Stella. Henry heard him whisper, "How's the training going?" to Stella.

"Grand," Stella whispered back and Henry saw that she flashed him a smile which, if it wasn't quite a 500 kilowatt beam, was certainly warming up to it.

The passengers in the back were all rather quiet. Those in the front, cheerful.

"Fine day for flying," said Mr Chancey. "Going far?"

"It might seem far to some," said Harvey Angell, "to those who know only clock time, not love time."

"You've got me there, guv," said Mr Chancey. "The sort of time I know is accordion time."

"Accordion time?"

"Yes. Time all squeezed up small, and Time stretching out long."

"Love time," said Stella Maris gazing

142

dreamily at Mr Chancey, "is the time you keep in your heart."

"'Love's not time's fool,'" quoted Mr Perkins from the back.

Aunt Agatha stretched out a foot to kick him and then tapped Mr Chancey on the shoulder. "Do you think you could possible *take* your time, and go a little slower?" she asked. "At this speed Sweetheart might well be sick."

"Certainly, darling," said Mr Chancey. "My time is your time." Mr Perkins looked out of the window and sulked.

Actually it was Aunt Agatha, not Sweetheart, who was in danger of being sick. Sweetheart, very alert and lively, played first with Henry's nose, trying to twist it off, and then with Mr Perkins' ear.

As for Henry, as they drove further and further out of town, he had the odd feeling of leaving his childhood behind and travelling into his own future. A future without Sweetheart. Perhaps without Harvey Angell.

As if reading his thoughts, Harvey Angell turned round and gave Henry the 500 kilowatt beam. "Just think, Henry," he said, "of all that love you've given Sweetheart whizzing into the twenty-third century. It won't be lost, you know. Sweetheart will take it with her."

Henry tried to smile back and failed.

Very soon they were out in the country. Mr Chancey stopped the cab by a meadow. At any other time, Henry would have thought it a

143

wonderful place for a picnic. The meadow danced with daisies, buttercups and cowparsley as delicate as lace. At one end it sloped towards a stream. And rising behind the meadow, hill upon hill stretched into the distance.

Once they'd unloaded the balloon from the trailer it became apparent why Harvey Angell needed their help. First they had to unfold the big blue skin of the balloon and lay it on its side. On the ground it seemed enormous.

"Now for the hardest part," said Harvey Angell. "We have to flap."

"Muggins is very good at that!" said Miss Skivvy starting to giggle. "Flapping, I mean."

"That's very rude," said Miss Muggins indignantly.

"Ladies!" said Harvey Angell. "*Please!*"

Flapping turned out to be hard work. Rosie sat on the ground with Sweetheart, testing her liking for butter with buttercups. The others held the mouth of the balloon and flapped air into it. It took so long that the sky began to cloud over while they were doing it and Harvey Angell looked worried.

"I don't think there's much air left in me," said Mr Perkins after about half an hour of flapping.

As the balloon slowly filled and puffed up, Harvey Angell lit the gas burner that went under the basket and produced a broom handle. "Someone's got to go inside and hold this up until the balloon's fully inflated," he said.

"Whoever does that is called Cremation Charlie," said Mr Chancey cheerfully.

"I suppose that's me, then," said Mr Perkins, taking the broom handle. "Into the mouth of the whale I go," he added, crawling inside that balloon as it now, slowly, began to right itself and to pull on its moorings.

Still more clouds gathered. Then Henry, looking up at the sky, saw it. A shaft of sunlight coming down the side of the hill and a figure slipping, sliding, running down.

"Wait! Wait!" he shouted. "Look!"

In total silence they all gathered to look where Henry pointed. Mr Perkins struggled out from inside the balloon. Miss Muggins and Miss Skivvy, suddenly afraid, clung together. Stella hid her face against Mr Chancey's shoulder. Sweetheart tried to free herself from Rosie's arms. Henry turned white as a sheet.

Just where the shaft of sunlight stopped and turned into shadow, the figure also stopped. It seemed to be fighting and failing to get through some kind of invisible wall.

"She's come!" said Harvey Angell, his voice hushed. "Henry, bring Sweetheart."

Like an automaton, Henry obeyed, lifting Sweetheart from Rosie's arms.

"Sweetheart's mother," said Harvey Angell, "She can't get any further. She's caught in the time gap. It's up to you now, Henry. You'll have to take Sweetheart to her."

"Me?" squeaked Henry.

"Yes, you. The one closest to Sweetheart and the youngest has the best chance. You're least time-freighted. You may have to push through the time gap. It may hurt. Go! Now!"

With Sweetheart in his arms, Henry began walking across the meadow. He could hear his heart booming in his ears. He could hear the faint hiss as the balloon began to deflate. He could feel the silent watching eyes on his back, and against his chest the dear, warm weight of Sweetheart.

Nearer and nearer to the bottom of the hill he came until the figure of Sweetheart's mother became clear. Clear enough for him to see her gentle face, her imploring eyes, her buttercup ears, her two tiny antennae.

At the place where the shadow ended and the light began, Henry suddenly felt all the tug of Time. It was like pitting his whole strength against a hurricane force wind. It made every step he took an enormous effort.

And then Harvey Angell was beside him, clearing the way, pushing back Time. Beating it. Together they were beating it. It felt to Henry as if the full power of Harvey Angell's 500 kilowatt beam had been turned into strength. Into Energy. And that Energy was now rushing through every limb and muscle of Henry's body. For minutes on end it was as if he was going to be torn in two. He felt the full force of Future Time hauling him forward and the full weight of Present and Past dragging him backwards.

And just at the moment when, mind blown, he felt outside all Time and without an ounce of strength left . . . Sweetheart and her mother took over.

Simultaneously they stretched out their hands towards each other. To Henry it seemed that Sweetheart almost leapt from his arms and into those of her mother's. And then for the first and last time, Henry heard Sweetheart speak. "Mama!" she said and they were both gone.

Henry collapsed on the ground. He could hear the others cheering and their feet running towards him before he blacked out.

CHAPTER 20

When he came round the sky was swimming, the trees moving and Aunt Agatha was holding him. As if from a great distance Henry could hear her asking, "Will he be all right?" And someone – who was it? – answering, "Yes, he's just got a bit of what you might call jet lag. Or maybe time lag."

It was Harvey Angell, of course, and in a few moments the sky stopped spinning, the trees stayed put and everything came into focus again.

"Did I do it?" asked Henry. "Is Sweetheart safe?"

"Safely with her mother," said Harvey Angell. "You were terrific, Henry." Henry caught Rosie looking at him as if she thought so too.

"But what are we going to do without her?" asked Mr Perkins. "Without Sweetheart." Sitting up, though still feeling woozy, Henry saw that Mr Perkins had his big handkerchief out and was crying.

It was catching. Miss Muggins was next and then Rosie. Aunt Agatha tried hard not to, but then gave in and allowed just one or two tears to trickle down her nose. Stella Maris cried in sympathy and even Mr Chancey had to clear the lump in his throat and blow his nose.

Only Henry didn't cry. Henry was remembering how Sweetheart had reached out to her mother, how she had spoken that one word, 'Mama' and how he had felt.

"I felt like Father Christmas," he announced to the astonished company. "That's how I felt."

"Are you *sure* he's all right?" asked Aunt Agatha anxiously. "His timing seems muddled up." And she felt Henry's forehead in case he was running a temperature.

"I felt like Father Christmas," Henry explained – as much to himself as to everyone else – "giving someone the present they most wanted in all the world."

"Henry, you're a dear fellow," said Harvey Angell. "And you're absolutely right. You have given Sweetheart what she most wanted in all the world. And now what I most want, is for everyone to cheer up. How about a balloon ride home?"

With the exception of Miss Muggins there was a chorus of "YES!" to this and within minutes they were back to flapping. Now that a ride was in view, they all flapped with renewed enthusiasm. Henry was told to rest. Mr Perkins went back inside the balloon with the broom handle. Harvey Angell re-lit the burner.

There was something magnificent about the

way the balloon came to life. How it began on its side and rolled over and upright, like a huge sleeping animal waking up. Its sky-blue sides grew fatter and fatter. It trembled as if with excitement. It lifted eagerly from the ground as if anxious to be off, surfing the thermals. Even Miss Muggins decided she couldn't miss out. "If someone holds my hand . . ." she said.

Then they all climbed in the basket. The burner was fully fired and with a dragon-like roar and a whoosh, up they went, Rosie clutching Henry and saying, "Oh Wow! Oh Wicked. Oh Brill, brill, brill!" Down on the ground Mr Chancey and Stella, waving at them, grew smaller and smaller.

"Are you sure you know the way?" Miss Skivvy asked Harvey Angell.

"You're forgetting," said Harvey Angell, "Homing is what I'm good at."

So after that they concentrated on enjoying the view, pointing out landmarks of rivers and churches and, when the balloon drifted low enough, waving. They waved to a farmer in his field, a woman walking her dog, a boy by a railway track.

"It's about one hundred thousand times better than being on a swing," shouted Rosie above the noise.

Henry was thinking how being up high changed your view of everything. How small houses and people looked. How worries big as double sheets, shrank small as hankies. Up among the clouds Henry felt he was in no-time – neither past, present nor future time. He thought about Sweetheart whizzing off to the twenty-third century taking their love with her. Yes, he thought, and she's left us lots here.

Soon they were flying over the town, Rosie almost hanging out of the basket and shrieking, "There's our school! Look! There's the park. And that – that must be the library!"

All of them together shouted, "Ballantyre Road!" as Harvey Angell gently and expertly brought the balloon down into the back garden of 131. And there was Mrs Sowerby running down the garden, working her arms like propellers and calling, "Air Traffic Control! Air Traffic Control!"

"Silly old bat!" said Aunt Agatha affectionately.

* * *

The house, without Sweetheart, felt as if the heart had gone out of it. There was that kind of silence of someone missing. They all felt it. Aunt Agatha put away the cot and the pram so as not to be reminded all the time. Miss Muggins washed and folded all the nighties and cardigans she'd stitched and knitted and took them to the charity shop.

But none of this helped them to stop missing Sweetheart.

"No-one to cuddle," said Miss Skivvy.

"Or take to the park," mourned Rosie.

"Or fuss over," said Miss Muggins.

Mr Perkins wrote:

> We miss her bleeps, we miss her smiles,
> We miss her miles and miles and miles.

But now that he was down on earth and back in the present, it was Henry who felt loneliest of all and who missed Sweetheart as if he'd lost an arm or a leg. Everyone tried to cheer him up. Mr Perkins suggested a game of cricket in the park. Mrs Sowerby baked his favourite cake. Rosie lent him her panda. The only people who didn't pay Henry any attention were Aunt Agatha and Harvey Angell.

These two spent long hours in earnest discussion at the kitchen table. Whatever they were talking about made the pins fly out of Aunt Agatha's hair and her face turn first red and then white as if summer and winter were coming and going very fast indeed.

Occasionally Henry heard her voice rise into a squeak of protest and drop into a groan. "The cost! The cost!" he heard and then came Harvey Angell's soothing murmur. Henry caught a couple of stray phrases – 'warm the heart', 'think of the future'. And once he heard Harvey Angell say, 'but Stella Maris will fix it.' What could *she* have to do with anything, Henry wondered crossly. But mostly Aunt Agatha and Harvey Angell went very quiet when anyone else came into the kitchen and this made Henry feel even more lonely.

Lonely, cross and left out, that's how he felt. Henry thought of Harvey Angell as his own Extra Special Friend. And now the only person Harvey Angell had time for was Aunt Agatha. The two of them had a secret and they weren't telling him. It was mean and unfair.

For once, going to school seemed better than staying at home. And when he did come home, there was Harvey Angell and Aunt Agatha (looking rather wild) sitting at the table with papers spread out between them. Letters and accounts and lists – all of them hastily hidden when Henry appeared.

Henry sulked. Took it out on Rosie. Slept badly. He woke in the night, looking for Sweetheart. And then he tossed and turned and there seemed to be a dozen voices in his head whispering, 'it's a secret, a secret, a secret.'

But what, Henry wondered every morning when he woke up, could it be?

CHAPTER 21

On Monday of the following week he found out. He was trudging gloomily home from school, head down, feet scuffing the pavement, bag of books banging his back, when he heard it – the sudden rush and roar of fire. Looking up Henry saw the big silver balloon, hanging almost directly above him and Harvey Angell leaning out, shouting and waving at him.

As Henry gazed up, Harvey Angell dropped down an enormously long kite string with a note tied on the end of it. Henry pulled it off, opened it up and read:

HAVE LEFT YOU LOTS OF SWEEHEARTS. HAVE FUN.
LOVE YOU ALWAYS. H.A. xxx

Dropping his book bag on the ground, Henry looked up again. The balloon was pulling away, rising over the house tops. Even at this distance Henry thought he could tell that Harvey Angell was smiling, sending down one of his big 500 kilowatt beams full of Energy.

Henry waved his arms wildly and ran home as fast as he could, the note clutched in his hands. 'Lots of Sweethearts'! What on earth could that mean?

Outside the front door the white hollyhocks that flourished only as long as Harvey Angell was in the house, had vanished. In their place were new blue hollyhocks, yellow hollyhocks, purple hollyhocks all jiggling together as if they were playing Chinese whispers and passing a message from flower to flower.

Henry barely had time to notice them because there was such a noise coming from inside the house. A noise like a party. And inside the house it grew even louder.

It came from the sitting room. Henry opened the door and a dozen small faces turned to look at him. Babies of one month, two months, three. Tots and toddlers, and the sitting room itself – transformed.

Harvey Angell's bed had gone and so had the sofa and chairs. In their place was a play pen, a baby bouncer, a plastic sandpit, a big dolls' house, a table of paper, paints and crayons, a book corner, lots of bean bags, two cots, three high chairs and a colourful notice on the wall that said:

BALLANTYRE ROAD CRECHE AND PLAY SCHOOL.
(WAIFS AND STRAYS BRANCH)

And right in the middle of it all, singing a sea chanty to a circle of tots, was Stella Maris. Stella looking star bright. Stella smiling at Henry like a Homer at home.

Dazed and dazzled Henry looked about him. There was Mr Perkins (making sandpies instead of poems), Miss Skivvy (with paint on her nose and three tiny artists waving paint brushes in the air), Miss Muggins (contentedly bouncing a baby on her knee), Rosie (singing to another one) and Aunt Agatha . . .

Well, Henry could hardly believe his eyes. Aunt Agatha was sitting on the floor with one small boy in her lap and another beside her building a tower of bricks. And what made Henry's mouth open in a huge O of astonishment was not so much the wonderful playground that the sitting room had become, but that he had never seen his Aunt looking so happy.

It was as if all Aunt Agatha's wintery withers had blown away forever and ever. It was as if, at last, she was set free from sorrow, as if she was all summer and flowering, flowering like the hollyhocks.

Aunt Agatha looked up and grinned at Henry. "Welcome home, Henry," she said. "Thanks to Harvey Angell and Stella Maris, here, we've become Registered Cuddlers!"

"You see," said Stella, "when Homers are out on their Homing Assignments they need Cuddlers to care for their children and Harvey Angell asked me to fix it."

"To be Cuddler in Chief," said Aunt Agatha, "with us to help her."

Henry grinned at them both. He could almost hear the echo of Harvey Angell's voice murmuring, 'warm the heart', 'think of the future'. And his own heart suddenly felt as warm as if Harvey Angell's 500 kilowatt smile, was shining inside him.

A tot with a bright red bow in her hair toddled unsteadily towards him and clutched his knees.

Henry swung her up into his arms.

"Hello, little one," he said. "Aren't you a sweetheart!"

Harvey Angell

By Diana Hendry

The stranger was a small, neat man. He had soft fair
hair the colour of thatch, a rather long nose and
eyes that might have been green and might have
been blue and might have been grey. All you could
truly say about them was that they were changeable.
He wore denim dungarees - brightly patched at the
knees - and carried a canvas tool bag.

"Henry," said Aunt Agatha, "I want you to meet our
new lodger, Mr Harvey Angell."

*Harvey Angell arrives at Ballantyre Road and lights up
the drab lives of Aunt Agatha, Henry and their lodgers.
No ordinary handyman, when Harvey's around the
atmosphere's electric! Henry decides to find out
the truth about the new lodger and discovers
what Harvey's real mission is!*

Winner of the Whitbread Award
**'A lovely book - funny, imaginative
and both clever and comforting.'**
Sunday Telegraph

Red Fox £3.99
ISBN 0 09 925602 9

Harvey Angell and the Ghost Child

By Diana Hendry

"Did you...?" he began.

"Yes," said Henry. "Did you...?" He wondered if his own face was as pale as Mr Perkins'.

"I thought I saw..." said Mr Perkins. It was as if he might make the ghost child real if he put her into words.

"Are you thinking what I'm thinking?" asked Mr Perkins after a long silence.

"I'm thinking," said Henry, as carefully as if his voice might break the glass, "that we need Harvey Angell,"

"Snap!" said Mr Perkins.

When Aunt Agatha books a summer holiday, Henry imagines lounging by the seaside and eating ice-cream everyday. But the reality is a rain-soaked fishing village and the forbidding Sibbald House, where Henry can sense a mystery hovering in the air. The eccentric landlord and the villagers will not answer any of Henry's questions. So when the mystery finally reveals itself, Henry realises that this is a job for his friend, the magical Harvey Angell.

'**Harvey Angell is one of the most engaging characters to emerge from children's fiction for a long time.**'
Bestseller

Red Fox £3.99
ISBN 0 09 922052 0